Murder's Out of Tune

An Amicus Curiae Mystery

Published by ECW PRESS
2120 Queen Street East, Suite 200, Toronto, Ontario, Canada M4E 1E2

LIBRARY AND ARCHIVES CANADA CATALOGUING IN PUBLICATION

Miller, Jeffrey, 1950–
Murder's out of tune / Jeffrey Miller.

(An Amicus Curiae mystery)
ISBN 1-55022-703-3

I. Title. II. Series: Miller, Jeffrey, 1950– . Amicus Curiae mystery.

PS8626.I45M88 2005   C813'.6   C2005-903325-8

Cover and Text Design: Tania Craan
Cover illustration: Gordon Sauve
Production and Typesetting: Mary Bowness
Printing: Marquis Book Printing

This book is set in Solstice and Garamond.

With the publication of *Murder's Out of Tune* ECW Press acknowledges the generous financial support of the Government of Canada through the Book Publishing Industry Development Program (BPIDP), the Canada Council for the Arts, and the Ontario Arts Council, for our publishing activites.

Canada   Canada Council   Conseil des Arts
          for the Arts   du Canada

DISTRIBUTION
CANADA: Jaguar Book Group, 100 Armstrong Avenue, Georgetown, ON, L7G 5S4

UNITED STATES: Independent Publishers Group, 814 North Franklin Street, Chicago, Illinois 60610

ECW PRESS
ecwpress.com

Murder's Out of Tune

An Amicus Curiae Mystery

JEFFREY MILLER

ECW PRESS

Also by Jeffrey Miller

Murder at Osgoode Hall, 2004

Where There's Life, There's Lawsuits: Not Altogether Serious Ruminations on Law and Life, 2003

Ardor in the Court: Sex and the Law, 2002

The Law of Contempt in Canada, 1997

Naked Promises: A Chronicle of Everyday Wheeling and Dealing, 1989

To my cousin, Lou Chapman, for a
childhood generosity I can never altogether
repay — trusting me, alone at Gramma's
house, with his red-hot Gibson SG and
his pawnshop tube amp.

And, in memory of Paul Emil
Breitenfeld, a Des Cheshire lookalike,
and occasionally sound-alike, but otherwise
an altogether different cat.

"Not Cassio kill'd! Then murder's out of tune,
And sweet revenge grows harsh."
—*Othello, on learning that his rival Cassio lives on,*
Othello *V, ii*

"This contract is so one-sided, I'm surprised
to find it written on both sides of the paper."
— *Attributed to the English judge, Lord Ellenborough*

A portion of Tommy Profitt's "stand-up act" appeared, in a different form, in *The Lawyers Weekly*. The goodwill cases Amicus quotes are genuine, and available in the publications he describes. His mini-biography of Dick Whittington also comes from actual human sources, notably *The Dictionary of National Biography*.

CONTENTS

SECTION A
'Til Death Us Do Part
(Allegro ma non troppo)   1

SECTION B
Dead at the Chicken Alley
(Andante e cantabile)   83

SECTION C
(FINALE)
Seems like Old Times
(Allegro con sentimento)   203

'Til Death Us Do Part

(Allegro ma non troppo)

CHAPTER 1

Things Ain't What They Used to Be

How Many of You Are There in the Quartet? That was the title of a book Des Cheshire kept threatening to write. He got the idea, he said, from the question airline attendants asked him as he travelled with Billy Wonder from gig to gig around the world: "And how many of you are there in the quartet?" But now it was no joke. Suddenly, the answer was three — now that Billy Wonder sat slumped against the piano, with two drumsticks hanging off the wire twisted around his neck.

In twenty-eight years of touring, their show had never opened quite so dramatically. Tommy Profitt, the comic, had warmed up the crowd as he normally did when he wasn't too juiced to go on. As usual, he had performed in front of the curtain on the bandstand, perched on a stool, brandishing the morning's newspaper. When Tommy finished his angry intellectual act, Jersey Doucette shook his head in practised disgust, looking like he could just about keep himself from spitting on his floor, and picked up the microphone he kept behind the bar. He snapped the mic on with a loud pop, breathed sonorously into the sound system, then mumbled in his wet and gravelly *basso profundo*, "And now, ladies and gentlemen, in their exclusive two-week run at the Chicken Alley in the heart of glamorous Yorkville, ringing in this brand new year of two thousand and five with their timeless cool-jazz stylings, a warm welcome, please, for our feature attraction, the Billy Wonder Quartet."

It was like the voice of God, but on codeine.

Popping the mic off, Jersey pressed the doorbell switch mounted under the bar's ledge and the motor on the automatic curtain stuttered into action like a used-up electric cake-mixer. Briefly. As usual, Jersey had to hike over to the stage and give the mechanism a manual assist, getting a bigger laugh from the packed club than Tommy had managed during his entire routine. Jersey pulled the curtain wide to reveal Billy spot-lit at the piano. The rest of the stand was dark, but if you squinted you could just make out in silhouette Jimmy 'Bones' Whitehead at his bass, Terry Denver on drums, and Des — aloof, standing a little removed from the three others — holding his alto sax at the ready. Yet something like deer-jacking was in the air of Jersey's little uptown nightclub, intensely white-lighted indicators that the evening was seriously off kilter. Billy was slouched over the old Steinway like he'd had three Singapore slings too many. If you were sitting near the front you could have heard Des remark, "Reminds me of the guy who asks, 'Hey, bartender, do you serve zombies?' and the bartender says, 'Sure, what'll you have?'"

What you didn't hear was Billy's usual command before the quartet launched into their big hit, "The Big Band Theory of the Universe." "Play like hell or I'll kill you," Billy always said, before counting the 5/4 opener in to cheers of recognition. Instead, tonight you would have heard Terry laugh in the dark as the bow from Jimmy's bass moved into the spotlight to nudge Billy, who responded by slumping solemnly towards the audience, banging out a dissonant E-flat minor seventh as his forearm and head slipped off the soundboard onto the Steinway's keyboard. As the house lights came up, Billy toppled head first to the floor, the piano bench slowly tipping the opposite way behind him, then hitting the stage with a decisive bang and spilling Jersey's collection of vintage *Playboy* magazines from under its lid. Just before Billy fell, you could quite clearly see the drumsticks dangling from his neck — like, Des would later say, "the big old tacky earrings on your average wired streetwalker."

Of course it was his penchant for gallows humour that would help earn Des Cheshire some rather pointed critical attention. And that attention would bring Yours Now and Then Truly, along with my occasionally faithful companion, Theodore Elisha Mariner, Justice of Appeal, to Des Cheshire's defence.

How His Lordship and I had ended up at Toronto's Chicken Alley is a blood-and-guts melodrama in itself. When he was in law school, Justice Mariner had waited table for Jersey — waited table, bussed table, swept the floors, cleaned the toilets, mopped the puke, pincered the hypodermics and condoms off the restroom floors with the fry chef's tongs, chauffeured drunken musicians back and forth between their hotels and their gigs at the Alley, and intervened in fisticuffs, lovers' quarrels, and the occasional cat or racoon fight among the garbage cans out back. The budding lawyer had found himself (in other words) on general, all-around clean-up in the down-and-dirty little tavern fronting the laneway running between Yorkville Ave. and Cumberland near Bay. Then, too, there were the evenings when the band didn't show up at all and, with the patrons getting restless and ready to hot-foot it, the callow law student was invited to show them what he could do at the ivories. Briefs, they called him, not necessarily because his girlfriend of the day had given him boxer shorts with the scales of justice printed on them, but probably because whenever they asked young Ted Mariner what he was doing with his school books spread all over the bar during his breaks he would shrug and reply, "The usual, just briefing the cases."

From then on, to fill the musical voids, it was "Hey, Briefs, show us what you can do." And a passable Fats Waller-style barrelhouse was what Briefs Mariner could do, as I can attest at first hand. Thirty-odd years later the gift's still more or less with him, along with his razor-sharp ear for the false note in an alibi, honed during a couple of decades' practice at the criminal defence bar.

Of course, Briefs Mariner's menial and musical days at the Alley were history long before the white-shoe developers and bomber-jacket impresarios gentrified Yorkville with condos and bistros and steakhouses. At least a decade passed before the little enclave of one-way streets filled with German luxury cars and the after-eight cokeheads who worked in the law firms and stock brokerages a few blocks south. In the older days, Jersey's crowd came by their *delirium tremens* and cold-sweat shakes in the same shirt and tie they had worn the day before — and the day before that, and the week before that — racking their ragged brains for where they could beg, allegedly borrow, or straight-out rip off the cash for their next fix and smoke. "And thank Providence for that," His

Lordship is prone to reminisce. "As one of my buddies on the garbage trucks said in those days, 'It might be shit to you, but it's bread and butter to me.' Those junkies, boozehounds, and wiseguys were my bread and butter. They helped me get my practice on its feet — them and their legal aid certificates."

As I have recounted earlier,* the judge and I hooked up when the staff at the Great Library of Osgoode Hall, seat of the province's Law Society and highest courts, rescued me, in their humble opinion, from the streets of downtown Toronto. No, I was not exactly one of the homeless and needy who wander into the soup kitchen in the Hall's basement cafeteria several days a week, to avail themselves of the Law Society's Feed the Hungry program. Indeed I am not even human or *Homo allegedly sapiens* — H.A.S. for short, or "Has-beings" as they are known among my own kind. As those of you previously acquainted with my legal adventures will recall, I am of the bar of *felis sylvestris*, laterally known as *felis catus* or, yes, a completely independent and self-reliant C-A-T for short. And I am congenitally equipped for life at the law courts, as though nature had fore-ordained it, in my robe of silken black fur, with the two white stripes running down my neck at a forty-five degree angle one to the other, just like the tabs the barristers wear with their black gowns in Osgoode Hall's courtrooms. And so, although I am not always popular with the habitués of the Hall, they have dubbed me Amicus, for *amicus curiae*, of course, friend of the court — or, in full, Amicus, Q.C., for Questing Cat, and your Quixotic Correspondent.

*See *Murder at Osgoode Hall*, 2004.

During the second year of my acquaintance with the judge, domestic strife entered life *chez* Mariner. His Lordship blames it on Mrs. Mariner's menopausal hormones. Penny (so Mrs. Mariner is called by her familiars) blames it primarily on His Lordship's choice of new law clerks, the otherwise highly recommended Nadia Hussein, second in her graduating class at Osgoode Hall Law School.

Nadia was somewhat younger than both Mariner daughters, the ethereal Claire, who recently had become a mother and was on leave as second-chair oboist with the Calgary Symphony Orchestra, and the more urbane Catherine, who was a chip off the old block but with polish — a high-flying corporate lawyer at a large and prestigious law firm on Bay Street. The upshot was that after the gardening and the cooking and the book club and the volunteer work at the Canadian Opera Company and the Frontier College literacy program were seen to, Mrs. Mariner — Penny — was at a loose end. Meanwhile, and I can vouch for this, His Lordship had begun spending even more hours at the office (judge's chambers these days, of course) than previously had been his habit in his many busy years at the bar. Whether this was because Penny suddenly had more time and inclination to pass judgment on His Lordship's conduct and character I cannot say for sure. Her view on things in general these days certainly was at least occasionally informed by hot flashes and mood swings, as she herself admitted. "I feel like one of those dying stars," I once heard the poor woman say in mid-flash, "going out with a whimper, her banging days being well and truly behind her." I believe Penny and one of the female judges were sharing mid-life war stories at the time, during some wine and two-bite quiche function at

Osgoode Hall. In any case, Penny Mariner lately had come to feel that, after three decades, His Lordship had given his fair share to his profession and public service, and it was time to balance out the ledger as paterfamilias and new granddad.

Truth to tell, His Lordship had chosen an unusually attractive young woman for this year's clerk. I will leave it to you as jurors, my readers, to decide on the evidence in what follows if the judge's choice of Nadia Hussein was a symptom of a mid-life crisis of his own (as Penny Mariner seemed to think), perhaps complementing, or in reaction to, his wife's passage across the threshold of menopause. Let it be said immediately, however, that if Nadia Hussein was a floozy, as far as I could tell she had little opportunity to practise that avocation. While the judge took her for the occasional lunch or drink, pending further investigation I must say that she was otherwise totally pre-occupied with research for His Lordship and the other appeal judges. And as you will see, she was a great deal more than an exotically pretty face. So all I can state for sure is that push inevitably came to shove, and, having jammed the contents of His Lordship's dresser into an old duffel bag — probably from the judge's law school days, in fact — Penny Mariner queried (as we say over at the Court of Appeal): "You prefer chambers with your twenty-something floozy night and day, day and night? Why bother to come home at all, then?"

As for me, well, my billet at the library had received one sniffy complaint too many from alleged allergy sufferers, and there was a similar problem *chez* Mariner. Mrs. His Lordship, a.k.a. the tarnished Penny, wouldn't have me in the house on the off-chance that daughter Claire, who was allergic herself, might want to bring the new baby, who could have inherited said sensitivity to feline dander. "I'm not taking the chance," Penny said one evening ante-bust-up, as His Lordship stood at the front door of their Upper Forest Hill abode, holding Yours Waifishly in the Humpty Dumpty potato chip carton the librarians had cut down for my bed. I vulnerably showed my belly, taking great pains to look absurdly unthreatening on the old grey army-surplus blanket in the box. But it was to no avail.

Bailiff, take the prisoners down to the cells!

Of course, as with my companion human, my record of previous convictions totted up against me: first-degree aviacide on the Hall's front lawn (I harvested a male cardinal whose comings and goings with its mate His Lordship had closely followed from chambers); vandalizing, in said chambers, the upholstery on an antique chair, formerly owned by John Beverley Robinson, 1791 to 1863, Attorney General and Chief Justice of Upper Canada for thirty-three years; recklessly or negligently or with undue regard for public safety tripping the current Chief Justice on the main staircase to the first floor (pure misadventure as I walked by on other official business, I swear it); going AWOL while in lawful custody; and similar, absolutely natural proclivities which the unjust Has-being considers criminal activity when engaged in by any other species.

Talk about giving a dog a bad name. Or, as His Lordship sums me up in one of his lamer attempts at humour: "His picture's next to the definitions for both 'mischief' and 'nuisance,' you know, in *Black's Law Dictionary*."

Assistant Librarian Katrina Slovenskaya, my official guardian at the library (and my official rescuer from death row in the Doghouse — the humane society shelter on River Street), had two cats of her own at home. So taking me in was out of the question for her good self. Probably I could have dossed down with one of the other librarians, or perhaps with someone working in the Law Society's education wing. But suddenly there was the judge alone and lonely after thirty-one years of cohabitation with the old Penny. How could I leave the ancient Mariner to fend for himself, after he had provided safe harbour to Yours More or Less Truly at Osgoode Hall?

I wouldn't go so far as to say that Jersey was understanding about our homelessness. However, after muttering and hemming and hawing and looking at his freshly mopped floor a few times (which had me woozy and teetering on all fours in the stench of bleach), he agreed that we could stay upstairs at the Alley for a while, he supposed, especially seeing how we were offering to pay him a hundred fifty bucks a week cash for his trouble — a C-note and a half, off the books, to sleep (we'd be lucky) on the torn-up, sprung-out old hide-a-bed couch that had been there since before His Lordship's law school days.

"Mind you don't be running up any kind of tab or nothing like that, neither, son."

Son. At fifty-something, and an appeal judge. "Wouldn't think of abusing your hospitality, Jers," we responded.

"And I suppose you'll be wanting to keep that critter in here with you." At this, Jersey nudged Yours Nearly Asphyxiated with his boot.

"Please," His Lordship replied, looking all apologetic like, sure enough, some big, soft kid. "He's not really such a bad old side-kick. And he'll keep your mice and cockroaches down to a dull roar."

Jersey threw him one of his trademarked bloodshot stares and said: "You telling me I got vermins in my bar, Briefs?"

His Lordship looked at the floor, scuffing his shoes. "Joke, Jers, just a joke. I'm just saying, you know, if you *did* . . ."

"He make any kind of a mess, the both of y'alls outta here like buckshot, just after y'all reimburses me for whatever he done. Fact, I'll be seeing your first month's rent up front as a damage deposit before I give y'all the key. That's the law, you know, Briefs."

Apparently nobody in the joint had heard of the presumption of innocence. His Lordship wrote a cheque.

"Hey, and Briefs?" Jersey said, inspecting the cheque closely between his sixteen-ounce sirloin hands.

"Yeah, Jers."

"I ain't got no vermins in my place. You dig?"

"Of course you don't, Jersey. No one knows that better than your old mop-boy. Clean as a whistle, or at least an alto sax."

Jersey shook his head. "Everybody's a comedian around my place." He gave us another look of disgust, which grew darker each hour that His Lordship spent in front of the television set above the bar during the next couple of weeks, seeking counsel from Judge Judy, Doctor Phil, and Her Majesty the Queen of Self Improvement, Miss Oprah Winfrey.

CHAPTER 2

Replaceable You

Arriving on Jersey's 9-1-1 call ("Yeah, I got a man down in my club, here, know what I'm saying? Personally, I wouldn't bother with no ambulance, though"), the first team of investigating constables and a sergeant meet Tommy Profitt, the comic, coming out of the club, shrugging himself into his brown leather bomber jacket trimmed with fake fur.

"We'll have to ask you to hang around for awhile, sir," the sergeant, a large man with a Vaselined brushcut, tells Profitt. Breathing heavily through his crushed nose, his body straining miserably against the seams of his herringbone suit and yellowed Arrow shirt, Det. Insp. Yastremski (as his badge says) looks uncannily like a big, colicky baby, and definitely not like the kind of person you want to argue with. Nonetheless, Profitt insists he has to be somewhere.

"We won't keep you long, sir," Yastremski responds, expressionless, blocking the doorway. Behind his bulging torso you can see a third marked police car arriving along with a paramedic's van (never mind Jersey's advice) and a fire chief's truck. The laneway is alive with the blue and red lightning of emergency signals, and the to-ing and fro-ing, at once bored and electric, of emergency personnel at work. Somewhere in the haze you can hear Jersey say, "Shit."

The Alley is still packed, but shock prevails. In the charged hush, conversation remains at a whispered minimum, all scaredy-cat fidgety, you might say, as the police circumnavigate the bar and tables, taking down the names and contact numbers of everyone present. They have drawn the curtains around the stage where Billy Wonder still lies near the fallen piano bench, his tongue blue between his teeth, sticking a third of the way out as you try not to stare at it. Then the cops allow most of the audience to leave.

Meanwhile, Profitt paces back and forth near the bar looking decidedly spooked, chain-smoking in the face of Jersey's advisory (in felt tip capital letters on the back of a grocery bag taped to the coffee urn) that the bylaws forbid it, casting furtive glances at the police as they work. "Cops," he says, to no one in particular. "Pigs," he adds, more quietly, blowing illegal smoke out his nose, showing his age.

When Detective Inspector Yastremski finally gets back to him, the detective brings along a note-taker, a young constable with acne at the edges of his short blonde hair. He looks much too skinny and innocent for police work in the Big Smoke. Shifting in his leather jacket, Profitt explains that he usually doesn't come to the club until about twenty minutes before he is scheduled to go on. "If I hang around before the show, I just get the heebie-jeebs, you know? Nerves." But on this particular evening, he was trying out some new material. And he wanted to make sure that when he was onstage with most of the lights down, he could read the cheater cards he'd taped to his newspaper. "I'd only just written the bit, see? It's untested, which is always a little dangerous anyhow. Edgy, dig?" So he came in about an hour and a half early to "prep" under near-live conditions. "Only it turned out I was near death." When no one laughs, which happens a lot to Profitt, it seems, he adds, "Just my luck."

"What do you mean by that?" the detective asks.

"I mean, it's just my luck that the night something like this happens, I'm hanging around the scene of the crime, breaking my usual pattern." Profitt lifts his hooded eyes, half-smirking, and studies the cop. "I mean, I guess that's how it looks to you, doesn't it?"

The detective takes a beat, gazing coolly back at his witness but giving nothing away. "What would you normally do in the fifteen or twenty minutes before you went on?"

"I don't know. You freshen up. Splash some water on your face. Check your clothes. Have a smoke. Get yourself hyped. You know, you go into your wiseguy mode. After I'd done the run-through, actually, I did go out for some smokes. Then up to the Indigo bookstore off Bloor, to browse, like, to kill time. Flip through the magazines."

"Was anybody else around the club until you went to the Indigo? Besides the bar staff?"

"Yeah. I remember noticing this girl sitting over by the wall, by herself, with her back to me, nursing a drink. I was p.o.'d about it, to be honest, because the place was supposed to be closed and I wanted to try out that new bit. So I did it anyway. She didn't even look up. Mutual abnegation society, as Des says of dead audiences. Should've told me something about the material right away, huh?"

Yastremski asks Profitt if he remembers exactly where the girl was sitting, and Profitt indicates a table well to the left of the stage.

All he can remember of her appearance is that she had black hair and was wearing a long, dark dress. "Sort of like a gypsy fortune-teller, or a ghost. A dark spirit. She creeped me out a little, actually. Like a bad omen."

"Anyone else around?"

"Just before I went out for my smokes, Billy came in to warm up. That was *his* usual routine. Besides the killer, I guess I might have been the last guy to see him, huh?"

"Could be. How did he look?"

"Same as usual. Made some lame joke about another day, another half-dollar. Then I went out, and, as I was saying, I had a coffee at the Indigo, a smoke outside." He stares at the fag end in his fingers. "I didn't come back until about, yeah, fifteen minutes before my act. Like I say, I get the jitters."

"And no one else was around before you left for the Indigo?"

"Now that you mention it, I think I saw Des — Des Cheshire, the sax guy in Billy's band." Profitt smiles broadly, but there is strain in his face. He has begun sweating, too, and his complexion is flushed. "Like me, he usually doesn't come in until just before he goes on. But I know he had to play on a cracked reed yesterday, and he was planning to come in early to buy some new ones, reeds, I mean, at Remenyi Music. Then I guess he might've wanted to work one in a bit, on his horn. Get set up."

"Remee . . ."

"Remenyi. The music store near Avenue Road. Just up Bloor Street, again. A ways up from the Indigo, on the opposite side of Bloor." Profitt takes a paper towel from a stack on the shelf near Jersey's card-table desk in the back office. He wipes his face, inspecting the perspiration on the brown paper. "Hot in here, eh?"

Yastremski blinks, but appears to be as comfortable as he might ever feel in a suit two sizes too small. "Did you see Des Cheshire out on the street?"

"Nope. But then I didn't have as far to go as he would have. Up Bloor, I mean. You know?"

"Anything else you can tell us that might help?"

Profitt wipes his face again and sits back, seeming to breathe more easily. His expression becomes less intense. "Well, I heard Jersey talking to someone in the back room. But that could have been just a delivery guy. Or maybe he was on the phone. Or cussing to himself, like he does all the time." Profitt laughs and shakes his head. "I really couldn't say."

"Thank you, Mr. Profitt. If you don't mind, I'll ask you not to discuss this with anyone else until we've finished our investigation. And we'd appreciate it if you'd hang around town for a few days. We'll probably need your help again."

"Hey, no probs, buddy." Profitt stands and winks at the hulking cop. "I'm supposed to be working here, anyway. Assuming somebody's still coughing up the bupkes old Billy thought I was worth paying, after all these years together." He shakes his head and laughs again, then looks contemplative. "Hey, you know, I suppose it'll be SRO after this, won't it?"

⚬〰⚬

The cops talk to His Lordship only briefly that night of Billy Wonder's death. I cannot report exactly what he tells them, as at that point I am otherwise engaged with janitorial duties, tonguing a trail of chicken-wing grease mingled with runny coleslaw mayonnaise,

Jersey's Six-Alarm Hot Sauce, and other gustatory succulents smeared along the floor as someone in the kitchen dragged a leaking garbage bag into the alley. I could add foreboding here by saying the trail looked like a long, smeary bloodstain, but truth to tell, it looked like barbecue sauce with mayonnaise in it. Anyway, given the evening's events, I have not otherwise dined, so preoccupied are my patrons with allegedly more pressing matters. Or at least that would be the generous interpretation of their gross neglect of the not-so-dumb domestic quadruped in their charge. I can recount, nonetheless, that at all relevant times before Billy Wonder took his final bow, His Lordship and I had an unobstructed view of said shocking event, seated as we were in Pervert's Row. That's what Tommy calls the front tables, adopting the lingo of the strip clubs that are his more usual habitat.

Being a long-time Des Cheshire fan, and having met him briefly while waiting tables in the Alley as a student, His Lordship had approached the front-and-centre table. Smiling and stepping lively to buck up his courage, he brandished a newly purchased CD remix of the Wonder quartet's 1968 classic, *Fellows in Wonderland*, which included the first release of the quartet's chart-topper, "The Big Band Theory of the Universe." The judge barrelled blindly on in — which is to say that, before he had a closer look and it was too late, Ted Mariner asked the alleged Des Cheshire to autograph the compact disk.

To be fair, the man wore a tweed jacket and old-fashioned (a.k.a. "retro") horn-rimmed spectacles something like Cheshire's. And, yes, he was sitting at the table normally reserved for the band members and their guests, just five or six feet from the stage, next to a strikingly beautiful woman who turned out to be Joy Almundy — the same Joy Almundy, late of Ottawa, now of Toronto, who enjoyed a minor celebrity as a sometime vocalist with the Wonder Quartet. She also claimed to have performed in session work with the likes of Tony Bennett and Frank Sinatra, but "We have yet to document this assertion," Cheshire has said of her, with a mock sniff. Almundy is a tiny thing of china doll beauty, freckled, brittle-looking, trim in a feline way, and her freckled décolletage was set off by the skin-tight dress she'd bought just that day, up the street at Holt Renfrew. Her face was carefully made up so that her bright red lips brought out her South Pacific Sea-green eyes. And she kicked me. Hard. Under the table. Twice. Screwing up her face tighter with each wallop.

One would not characterize Joy Almundy as the type who takes kindly to that old job description, "girl singer."

As I say, the faux Des Cheshire sat next to her. "Normal," Joyless Almundy called him more than once, pinching the loose skin of his arm and thigh (much harder in the latter case, I could tell, from my shin-view perspective), teasing him mercilessly as he smiled sheepishly into the void. Normal (or Normie, her other pet name for the poor sod) wore a tie knotted up to the very top of the collar of his white shirt, but you could detect severe razor burn on his throat, demonstrating that he had prepared assiduously for his date with the, uh, woman vocalist. Jersey's description of Normal later, in conversation with the judge, was, if you will pardon the expression, "pussy-whipped." It might sound speciesist, but I had to agree with the sentiment.

Startled at His Lordship's autograph request, Normal smiled up at him and said, "Uh, well, I'll sign it if you want, chief. But to be honest, I think it might devalue the thing for you rather than make it any kind of memento."

"I'm terribly sorry," the judge replied at this first opportunity to correct his mistake. "It's just that, from a distance, with your glasses and combed-back hair and all, well," he looked appropriately embarrassed, "I thought you were Des Cheshire. I mean, I know he's playing tonight, of course. But I can see now you're a youngster by comparison, aren't you? Up close and personal, as it were."

Almundy nearly killed herself and everyone else at the table laughing and slapping and pinching. Catching her breath, she took Normal's face in her hands and, between giggles, tearful eructions, and snorts of hilarity, managed to say, "Yeah, okay. If you cock your head and squint real hard, there's a slight resemblance, I suppose . . . in profile. *If* you squint. Hard. Jesus!" She put her arm around her boyfriend, and flapped her eyelids at His Lordship. "But you should know that *Normal* here's a bit of a square — an old fart before his time, *as it were*, up close and personal. Aren't you, sweetie?" She kissed said square on the cheek. "Des without the edge."

Edgeless Normal held out his hand to Justice Mariner and introduced himself: "Norman Clapham."

"Ted Mariner."

"Yes, the Owl and the Pussycat," Clapham replied with a bland smile, half-standing to shake hands.

"Sorry?" the judge asked.

"Have a sit," Morgan Denny, Billy Wonder's Canadian agent, said, kicking at the chair opposite him, pushing it out and banging its legs into mine. In the dark and din, of course no one noticed me as I now stuck close by my companion human, avoiding chair legs and Joyless's stiletto heels. It had been a couple of days of really being bounced around.

"I saw you the other day, at the bar with your cat," Norman Clapham explained. "You were feeding him cheese from your Ploughman's Lunch. You had your John Lennon-style specs on, wire-rimmed, with the round lenses, and you were reading. I thought to myself, 'They dined on mince and slices of quince, / Which they ate with a runcible spoon.'"

His Lordship laughed. "'And hand in hand, on the edge of the sand, / They danced by the light of the moon.'"

Clapham clapped his hands and finished, "'The moon, / the moon, / They danced by the light of the moon.'"

Joy Almundy made a face as though Clapham had farted stentorianly. But taking the proffered chair, a front-row seat in a sold-out house for the Billy Wonder Quartet, the judge patted his new friend on the shoulder. "What *is* a runcible spoon, anyway?" He was doing this a lot lately, striking up conversations with strangers in bars. I suppose it's what came of being mateless after so many years of domesticity.

Clapham blinked slowly, owl-and-pussy-cat-like, and responded, "Apparently it's a special fork, not a spoon at all. Used, I guess, for eating so-called rouncival peas. 'Runcible' is thought to be a corruption of 'rouncival,' you see. A deliberate, playful corruption, I suppose you'd say."

"See what I mean about square as cornbread?" Almundy broke in, pinching poor Clapham yet again. "Bor-ring!"

"It's amazing what you can learn in a bar," His Lordship said, shaking his head, sincerely taken aback, smiling at his new friends. "I'm really impressed. Particularly that a man of your relatively tender years can quote Edward Lear, let alone explicate him."

"Don't be too impressed," Almundy said, sinking her front teeth into the lemon-wedge from her vodka and tonic. "It's his job."

Taking his girlfriend's hand, which (as I could clearly see from under the table) she quickly withdrew, Clapham admitted, "I'm afraid Joy's right, as usual." He smiled at the singer and she beamed the compliment around the table, squeezing her eyes shut, grinning and otherwise looking as pleased with herself as if she'd just won a Grammy. "I'm finishing my doctorate at the U. of T. in Victorian social history," Clapham was saying, "the Industrial Revolution and all that. So I've had occasion to read some of the poets — Edward Lear, Lewis Carroll, you know."

"Well, I'm still impressed." The two men embarked on a long and, sure enough, terminally boring discussion of Martin Gardner's *Annotated Alice* (also of Wonderland), which conversation served as a Mickey Finn for Yours Somnolently, knocking me mostly out of action until Jersey's booming introduction of the quartet shook me back to my senses.

⁓◦◦⁓

Still, as I dozed and awakened, awakened and dozed, I could hear poor old Tommy Profitt trying to finish his turn on stage. As Jersey explained later to the cops, Billy had picked up the comic as an opening act because of the repertoire fit: like about half of Billy's playbook, a lot of Tommy's routine was stuck in the sixties, I guess, or maybe the fifties. Doubting Tommy, they call him, for his cynic's schtick. Knowing a trademark when he saw one, Profitt had used the sobriquet as the title of his second album, released in the nineteen-seventies. To increasingly limited success, he would come out with his newspaper — usually the city's main broadsheet; in this case, the *Globe and Mail* — and do his mongrelized Lenny Bruce, Mort Sahl, and Woody Allen thing, long, provocative, semi-intellectual riffs on politics, language, drugs, society, and sex. For the Chicken Alley gig, he'd developed that new material, gleaned, he said, from "too many years of playing this shithole." This particular line was not new, and every time he used it Jersey glared at him with his bloodshot, gluey eyes, leaning into the bar where he kept what he called his security staff: an old crowbar he'd found in the storeroom and a large French chef's knife, the kind with the curved blade for slicing through root vegetables and other tough customers.

As usual, casting his famously hooded gaze quickly over the packed room on this night of Billy Wonder's untimely demise, Tommy sneered gently, as though he really intended to smile, sitting mute until the audience discomfort grew palpable. Someone tittered nervously. Then Tommy started up abruptly in a deliberately hoarse, hushed tone, wetly suggestive — a little, Justice Mariner tells us, like the French sybarite and *chansonier*, Serge Gainsbourg:

Word got around and the Chicken Alley was SRO *by midnight. Old Billy, the faded Wonder boy of the eighty-eights, had just finished his second set and was sitting with Des Cheshire and a couple of used-up working girls, none of them saying much, eyeing the stage where the sales rep from the Music and Stereo Show was setting up his machine. The rep checked a patch and then called over to the table, "Kee doke. Ready when you are."*

Old Jersey had come over to collect the glasses, so he put his two cents in: "No way a machine can play as good as a man. Even a man that can't blow spit."

From up on the bandstand, the usually laconic Bones Whitehead said: "Shit."

The computer knew "Salt Peanuts," so they started out with that, the room going dead quiet with everyone waiting for the slightest clam, the rep standing to the side of the bandstand nearest his protégé, rocking slightly, his arms folded tight. There seemed to be general agreement that Des used his ideas with more taste and sensitivity, although the computer had come up with some pretty acute changes.

"Now try it on Duke," Jersey said, leaning on his bar and looking tired. They played a medley of "Satin Doll," "Don't Get Around Much Any More," and "Take the 'A' Train," and you could feel the fever in the place break. By the end there was a lot of noise and laughing and joking again, and some citizens took full drinking advantage of the after-hours — the idea being, as the smirking Cheshire Cat put it, "to hold off your hangover 'til it's time to start all over again."

"Yessir," Jersey agreed, dripping with sweat as he deked around the tables in the gloaming of his humid little bar, "say good morning to your nightcap." Even though he'd been muttering all night about the fire marshal and no after-hours licence, Jersey kept setting them up. Business was business, and he was minding his own. Some people had left, though, shrugging, reassured.

"Try it on 'Night in Tunisia,'" Julie the Junkie called out. It was one of those unusual occasions when the ageing transvestite spoke up, from her regular table off by the south wall where you could see into the laneway and wave at the dealers and the parking attendant out there in his shack. So some still say she put the hoodoo on in her long, black fortune-teller's lacy dress. "Double time," Julie said, so some blame her, see, the more so because she was supposed to be good friends with Des.

Waiting for Billy, hardly anyone attended to the angry, stoned-out comic. Most just talked over him with their table companions, wandered to the washrooms, ordered food and drink. Wiry Sylvie, Jersey's hardest-ass waitress — notorious for quitting every second day or so during all her six years at the Alley, insisting every time that it really was the last straw and she was packing up and heading back home to Quebec City — called out orders across the bar. Behind it you could hear Jersey ceaselessly clattering glasses, shovelling ice, popping bottle caps in Yorkville's black velvet night. A dark-eyed woman sitting against the west wall stared into her drink, mixing and remixing it with a plastic stir stick in the form of a sabre. A green sabre. She seemed oblivious to the January cold, although she wore a thin, dark-patterned cotton dress with little black straps, her upper chest bare and a little pimply, her shoulders covered with a lacy shawl. Periodically she wrote something in what looked like a leatherbound diary. The work was laboured, it seemed, as her long fingernails, tapered and painted dark purple, got in the way. Sitting in Perverts' Row, the beautiful if cruel Joy Almundy yabbered along at Norman Clapham, His Lordship, and the talent rep. Morgan Denny, preening and flirting among the men, oblivious to Profitt as he spun out the routine he had custom-made for the Chicken Alley. I awoke groggily to hear His Lordship ask Clapham if he knew anything about "the girl in black, by the wall there, the one who seems to be in here all the time."

Before Clapham could reply, Almundy crinkled her nose again as if something smelled and said, "That, Ted, is Normal's bosom buddy, the Stalker Kitten. He finds her so *mysterious*, don't you, Normal?" Almundy snorted. "She looks like something out of one of your Victorian novels. Mistress of Death."

"She must be rather pretty, though," His Lordship noted, "under all that war paint?"

"She is, actually," Clapham replied. "A lovely girl. And we just keep each other company, sometimes. I mean, sometimes I sit with her in the clubs or whatever when Joy's working. She's lonely herself, is all."

"She's always hanging around when Billy plays," Morgan Denny explained, darting a glance at the woman. "I mean, not just here. Everywhere. The chick seems to know him, but you seldom see her actually with him, or any of the other hangers-on." He looked briefly — inadvertently, it seemed — at Clapham and Almundy. "Sort of a lost soul, I guess."

"Not to mention fucking wonky," Almundy said. When Clapham made a wry face, she slapped at his chin and said in a mock baby-voice, "Oh-oh, we've offended wittle old Ab*Normal*ly Sensitive. Actually, Ted, as I've told Norman a bazillion times, if she's lonely, it's her own fault. Gianna and I, that's her name, as Norman well knows, Gianna Ravenscroft. She calls herself Kitten, which personally I find nauseating. Anyway, Gianna and I, we were friends, briefly. I tried, I really did. Out in L.A., after she'd pestered Billy so much about an audition, he said okay, thinking she'd go away after that. That's the only reason he knew her at all. It's the only reason *any* of us knows her at all. Suddenly one day, instead of sending him a tape, she shows up on Billy's doorstep, if you can feature it — looking all Gothy like that, as if she'd just arrived by time travel from the Black Death. Anyhow, we ended up in the same voice class out there, and we went for coffee afterwards, a couple of times. I mean, the woman moves to L.A., for God's sake, just to harass poor Billy."

Clapham smiled at his girlfriend, then at the judge. "Joy put Kitten straight on her singing before she wasted too much of her spirit. Joy told her she should maybe go the pop route, because she didn't have a jazz voice." Clapham chuckled and patted at Almundy's bare arm. She drew away with a look of mild annoyance. "So that was the end of that two-week friendship."

"Yeah," Almundy said, glancing briefly at the woman before waving her off as a topic of conversation, "and now she's probably got my name down on her witch's hit list. See that little black book she's got there, Ted?" Almundy sniffed. "She writes in it constantly, extravagantly tearing pages out of the thing, making a lot of noise about it when I'm singing or in the middle of Billy's solos. Trying to attract attention, as usual. I really think she's written our names down six hundred and sixty-six times each or something — the devil's number, you know — so she can cast them into a fire and we'll burn in Hell."

Clapham laughed. "Oh, come on. She's harmless. A perfectly gentle soul, and you know it."

Almundy snickered. "Yeah, well, the only remarkable thing about Gianna Ravenscroft is how unremarkable she is. Harmless? Maybe. But I'm telling you I'm in that black book, on her hit parade, the only one she'll ever know. Probably got a special curse reserved for me personally."

Yes, and who's egocentric now?

Clapham kept smiling, shaking his head. "She's lonely is all, ab-*normal*ly sensitive, artistic. And she's quite intelligent, by the way."

Through all of this, Profitt didn't bat an eye. He went on with his bit, louder and louder, pushing the general din higher and rougher.

Bones on bass and Billy the Wonderboy on the Yamaha baby grand flew into "Tunisia" like the place had caught fire and they were under strict contract — faster even than Bird played it at Massey Hall in '53. When Des Cheshire was only halfway through the alto break, less, even, the people cheered, stomped their feet, hollered, danced, hooted. "Hey, keep it down!" Cueball Finkelstein bawled out from the audience, then yelled himself hoarse: "Go! Go!" He was having wild ideas about the secret recording he was making against the Musicians' Union rules, trying on album titles: Shootout at the Chicken Alley, It's Wonder Who's Kicking 'Er Now, Medium and Message.

It turned out Cueball didn't have to worry about too much ambient noise because, when the computer took its solo, the place went drop-dead quiet again. That computer was all over the map, see, double the already double time, faster than you could take it all in. When it played an arpeggio it seemed to spout whole bouquets of notes, geysers of them, volcanoes of cool, smoking lava. Everybody kept expecting the thing to explode or something, because it didn't seem there was anywhere else for it to go. Not at that speed, anyway. No human could have puzzled out the changes it assembled, a furious dance of molecules, whirlwinds of them. No fingers could have moved at anywhere approaching that speed, the speed of light. No human lungs could have withstood it.

Finally, someone cracked: "Blowin' SMOKE!*"*

"Testify!"

"Bird is DEAD*, man!"*

"Would you check out the random access memory on that!"

Wonder and Cheshire jabbed back with "Perdido" and then uppercut with mysticism — "Giant Steps," "Naima," and some Sun Ra stuff, but the computer was just as weird, if not ten times obtuser.

Wonder anyway tried to go one better with Ornette Coleman, "Lonely Woman," "Una Muy Bonita," and then free-jazz, really far out changes on "Embraceable You," "Hipadel-phia," "Ko-Ko," "Tea for Two" as they might play it on other planets. The computer was still laying down "Cherokee," piano and tenor parts, both.

Cheshire put his horn away and, the bags under his eyes suddenly looking like gunny sacks, he declared, "I'm taking the standing eight count, boys, and the 'A' train out of this town, to boot." And he walked. No one had ever seen him on the street that early in the p.m, and without his horn, besides, but damned if he didn't leave it there on the bar, like a jilted lover. Still, business is business, and old Jersey held the new group over ("Corporate reorganization," was all Jersey said whenever anybody asked, but everyone knew about the pock-marked men in overcoats who spent five or ten minutes in his "office" in the storeroom behind the bar and didn't hang around to see if Sonny Rollins might show up that night). Wonder's group was now led by the computer synthesizer and called the Improvitron II Quintet after it. The quintet even got a month's worth of gigs along the coast, right away, and Ahmet Ertegun signed them to record at Atlantic Records. The technological revolution, I guess you'd call it.

About then, Terry Denver, Billy Wonder's drummer, and the bassist Jimmy Whitehead came and sat at Almundy's table in Perverts' Row. Almundy glowed, her full little décolletage flushing and rising higher in her dress, her eyes fluttering with confused pleasure as she struggled to decide which way to flirt next. But Jimmy Whitehead seemed immune to her charms. So she focussed her most determined efforts on him, pinching and poking at poor smitten-looking Norman all the while.

Everyone missed the Billy Wonder Quartet, of course, Tommy

Profitt went on. *But its time had come and gone. It was time to Take Ten, if you know what I mean — ten years of retirement in Boca Raton. The computer wrote a slow blues homage to Billy called "Replaceable You," the other bookend, you might say, to go with Cheshire's 1957 tribute, "S'Wonderfuller." And even Cueball Finkelstein had to admit the machine had more interesting ideas, never blew a clam, and never fit a squeaky reed. Terry Denver said it was better-natured than Des Cheshire, and better looking, too.*

It was good and steady for old Jersey's business, besides. He eventually hired the new quartet as his house band and pretty soon every musician in the country, and even some from foreign jazz hot spots like Denmark and Poland and Japan were coming to the Chicken Alley to check it out. Sonny Rollins showed, too, Cueball claimed. The rashest pilgrims stayed after hours and tried to cut the computer, but it was always the same John Henry situation, man against pile-driver.

And I suppose you figure the end of the story must be that one day the old lion Desmond Cheshire returned to the scene and restored his manhood, wiped Old Jersey's booze-and-blood-soaked hardwood floor with that over-heating s-box of Radio Shack refuse. And if you figured something along those John Henry lines, well, you're not far wrong. . . .

Billy might have heard the bit in rehearsal, of course, but if it was meant to get up Des's nose, as well, it was unlikely he had been in the bar for more than the tail end of it. Then again, maybe that was plenty — enough for Des to know that Tommy was labelling him and his colleagues a bunch of has-been Has-beings in the age of pop-rock and hip-hop.

Of course, as the night wore on, what Billy thought was quite literally neither here nor there.

CHAPTER 3

I Say Banana, You Say Tomato

"You own this joint?"

"You talking about my business here? My bread and butter? Is that what you might be referring to with your terminology of 'this joint'?" Jersey and Staff Inspector P. Gullion (his i.d. says) sit at a table about twenty feet from the bar, under which Your Vigilant Correspondent lies dozing on a crate of Perrier Single Servings/ *Eau minérale en petites bouteilles*

"This bar. Do you own it?"

Jersey looks frankly at the staff inspector, refusing to be intimidated, scratching his chin. "Jeez, officer. After thirty years, I can tell you in all sincerity, Inspector, sir, who owns my . . . *joint* . . . is the bank is what still owns it, yessir, lock, stock, and beer kegs. And days like this, it's damn well welcome to it, too. Uh-huh."

"What can you tell us about what happened concerning Mr. Wonder yesterday?"

"Nothing more than anybody else already told you that was in my bar when the curtain opened. However reluctantly. And by reluctantly I mean the curtain and me both. Neither of us got the will no more, tell you the truth."

"But as far as you know, Mr. Doucette, did Mr. Wonder have any enemies?"

Jersey rolls his eyes. "Ever'body's got enemies, Inspector. Even you, I imagine. Even us nice and smiley folks in this here clubs business. Lotta whadayacall — ego. Big heads, you know. I got the blood all over the tops of my doorframes here to prove it, see what I'm sayin'?" Both men look up, as though Jersey means it literally.

"Do you know of anyone in particular that Mr. Wonder didn't get along with?"

"Well, speaking of ego and attitude, I heard him and Tommy getting' into it more than once. But that's because Tommy's a damn cokehead and he don't put in no appearance half the time for his gigs. I've had words with him, myself. Told 'im that no-show business, it ain't no show business, see what I'm sayin'? The customers take it out on your venue, see, permanently, too. And anyway, you can't handle your shit, you don't do it, dig? You a professional. You let people down, you out of a job. There's plenty others grateful for the chance. Billy felt the same way."

"Tommy." Gullion makes a note in his little notebook. As he bends his head to write, you can see that his hair is neatly crew-cut, and the skin of his neck is girlishly white. As if in compensation, he has five o'clock shadow well before lunch, from his cheeks to the base of his throat. "Tommy who?" Gullion looks bleary-eyed, like he needs a stiff drink. But that's the usual condition of many of the Alley's patrons, as Jersey calls the customers he tolerates.

"Tommy Profitt. The so-called comedian. When Billy's in town, Tommy opens for him. And when he's clean, sometimes Billy takes him on tour. But he never be clean for long. That's what I'm sayin'. And he really pushes it with Billy. Ragging on Billy something awful."

"How do you mean 'ragging on Billy'?"

"It's just the way he is, with everybody. He makes — made, I guess I gotta say, poor ol' Billy — Tommy made fun of Billy in his routines. How Billy's the white elephant of jazz, and sounds like it, besides. 'It don't mean a thing, 'cause old Billy can't swing.' That kinda smart remarks. Old tunes, old hat. But people say it about the whole band, too, you know."

Yes, Tommy seemed to favour that particular theme. I'd heard him perform variations of it more than once. He'd talk about Billy being the latest in a long line of white dudes literally horning in on the African-American man's bread and butter. As if Tommy himself weren't ofay.

The first guy to see the real commercial potential in the jazz racket, shit, he was even named *Whiteman, dig? Paul* White-man, *dig, took jazz and bleached it out, fucking whitewashed it, man, making it safe for the middleclass* WASPs *waving their asses around at church suppers, doing the old foxtrot and the two-step waltz, you know? [Billy dances around the stage, singing, "It don't mean a thing 'cause dem honkies can't swing."] And now, today, we got my man, Billy Wonder Bread, pulling the same scam, on a higher plane. Billy Clorox, bleaching jazz whiter than white, doing the old Michael Jackson on the Duke, only for the ofay college crowd. The Great White Dope. [Sings:] "It don't mean a thing, 'cause poor Billy can't swing." I mean, dig this, folks. You know what's the motto at Billy's recording company? Dig: "If it ain't Baroque, don't mix it."*

"Billy hated that shit," Jersey says. "He said it was racist and he told Tommy to quit it. But Tommy just kept on at it, rag, rag, rag.

The kids liked it, but it was a old bone between them, Tommy and Billy, you know? And then that girl bounced between the two of them, too, Almundy, when she wasn't flirting with Des or someone else all the time." Jersey shakes his head. "And the madder Billy got at Tommy, the more Des kept fanning the flames, besides, for his own amusement, I guess, the three of 'em hissing and spitting like some alleycats. Like this troublesome ol' tomcat here lazin' around behine my bar, see? I mean, Des ain't nasty like Tommy, but they both teased Billy something awful, the way people do, in groups, packs, you know. Des was no fan of Tommy's, but they agreed pretty well on Billy's playing, see what I'm sayin? Des even wrote a tune, just to get in Billy's face about it. "Whaddaya Mean 'We,' Whiteman?" is what Des called it. And right in the middle of it he plays the main theme from "It Don't Mean a Thing," you know, the main lick. I mean, it's true enough, Billy never really *could* swing, poor bastard. But you don't say it to his face, do you Inspector? Des went and recorded the tune with Jim Hall on the guitar anyway." Jersey shakes his head with a wheezy laugh. "Yeah, it was pretty damn funny, I guess, but it pissed Billy off somethin' awful."

"Mr. Cheshire pissed Billy off, you mean?"

"Yeah, sir. Des. Mr. Cheshire. Like I say, he enjoyed ragging old Billy, too, Des did. Uh-huh."

"Anybody else had run-ins with Billy?"

"We been over that, I thought. Billy was a bandleader, Inspector. Combination boss, mama, daddy, priest, dealer, pimp, and whatall. He hired and fired people, like Joy, for instance, and Tommy, more than once or twice. He rode their ass to get their chops right, because it was his ass on the line, don't I know it? He yelled at them to get their ass in gear before they missed their plane, train, and bus. He was a big celebrity, too, you know. Hit parade and all that bunch o' nothin'. People kiss his behind to stab him in the back, you dig? The biggest white man on the popular jazz scene. The White Elephant of Jazz. Hell, biggest of any colour, never mind he's no Duke Ellington. But he was on the hit parade and all that, in the sixties, anyhow, and he was a good draw for the club scene. And not just jazz clubs. Yeah, a guy like that, a certain number of folks, a goodly number of 'em, I'd say, they think he's a prick, like, see what I'm sayin'? Mm-hmm, and excuse my *français*, the language of my ancestors. Billy had that reputation, but it goes with the turf, dig. And the money was good when he was in the neighbourhood, plenty of pretty girls was always hanging around, whether they had husbands or boyfriends or they didn't. So the players didn't mind gigging with him, you know? He was no worse than most in his position, you ask me. I mean, you heard the stories about, I don't know, Buddy Rich. Uh-huh. Stan Getz beatin' up on his beautiful super-model wife, robbin' a drugstore for his dope money, the fool. You got a better idea, I'm sure, Inspector, what's the matter with them boys than I do. Seems to me the white leaders got the worst reputation for it. I mean, yeah, Billy was reaming out Bones just yesterday about missing a cue or something, you want a for instance. But that was business. Shit, it don't mean a thing to *nobody*. Least of all to Jimmy. Billy was the boss and it was just — business. I wouldn't o' remembered it, myself, you wasn't asking."

"And who are these people, Bones and Jimmy?"

"Bones *is* Jimmy, dig? Jimmy Whitehead, the bass player in Billy's band. We call him Bones on account of he's so skinny. Don't mean nothing. Jimmy wouldn't hurt a fly. It went in one ear, out the other, believe me. I mean, even Billy and Des, they been together over twenty years, and far as I know they hardly exchanged two words in the last ten. It's like an old marriage, see what I'm sayin'? There's good, there's bad, but when you add it all up, two grumpy old heads is better than one, I guess. They need each other — Billy did the business, Des could just blow and be cool, you know, amble on in like the hotshot musician, the prima donna, and he go have a drink while Billy paid the bill and ordered up the cab. Just like an old marriage, they hung together 'cause one, you know, like complements the other . . . which, as a matter of fact, is what I just been trying to impress on my lodger, here, Inspector. Maybe you know him from your work? Mr. Justice Mariner, of the Ontario Court of Appeal. Mm-hmm. Staying upstairs with me. He's an old friend of mine, as it happens. Wife throw'd him out of his own house." Jersey stops briefly to contemplate this with a glint and a chuckle. "Mm-hmm. Thinks he's fooling around with his new law student or some such." Jersey shakes his head with a quiet little wheezy laugh, eyeing the cop closely, studying the effect of his sudden decision to drop old Briefs Mariner, his protégé who just happens to be an appeal judge, casually into the investigation.

Confirming Jersey's worst suspicions about His Lordship and Yours Narratively, Staff Inspector Gullion remains unimpressed. "And how did you get along with Mr. Wonder, yourself?" he asks.

Jersey stands, putting his hands up, his eyes wide. Slowly backing away, he says, "Okay, okay. You got me, Ossifer. I confess I done it, with my own bare hands. They's blood all over 'em, see? Wouldn't warsh off. I killed an act that'd sell out my joint for two weeks solid, even though it was just the third night they was in town. It's my genius for bankruptcy made me do it! I killed Billy Wonder, the great white mope! Case closed!"

"Mr. Doucette, I'm not your banker. I'm just trying to find out what happened."

"Shit. Maybe I had a million dollars *in*surance on poor Billy's sorry-ass neck. Maybe I'm the principal whaddayacall, benefisheeary, in his will or something. Mm-hmm. That's what ol' Des would call 'lipidinous happenstance — fat chance in the vernacular.'"

Inspector Gullion looks at Jersey like he doesn't need this crap.

"Yeah, all right." Jersey shrugs. "We had our discussions, I guess, Billy and me. But we got along all right. I hired him to play in my . . . *joint* . . . , didn't I just? We both got businesses to run, and we both been around a long time, Inspector. Or we *was* around a long time, I guess. Anyway, both of us knew that being the boss is not a popularity contest, see what I'm sayin'? And the jazz game, it's like the Battle of Iwo Jima, dig?, at the best of times. You need all the reinforcements you can find, you gonna plant that damn flag at the top of the hill. See what I'm sayin'? You don't make no enemies you don't need to make. Uh-huh. Some of ums got wire they gonna twist like a pretzel around your sorry-ass neck."

⌀⌀⌀

Once Jersey and Gullion have finally managed something approaching an exchange of information, the inspector explains that the best way to determine who killed Billy Wonder is to work backwards from the discovery of the crime. On that strategy,

Inspector Gullion asks Jersey when was the last time he had seen Mr. Wonder.

"I don't know. Just before he went out for supper, I guess. He always come down five-thirty, six, to use the piano. You know, like I say, get his chops up. 'Stretch out the metacarpals,' the way he put it. There's an old upright in one of the rooms upstairs, but it's in pretty rough shape. Just like the old management."

"And what time do the doors open?"

"Seven-thirty," Jersey says. "We open from eleven to four, for drinks and lunch, but then we close up again until seven-thirty."

Gullion asks if Jersey ever allowed anybody in after lunch closing but before seven-thirty.

The staff is under orders, Jersey explains with exaggerated patience, not to let anybody in except the musicians or delivery people, and Jersey often checks the doors himself to make sure they're locked again, especially because the bar staff is always going in and out to clean the place or to do their own business, or they're opening up for deliveries. "You get all types wandering in here off the street. Don't matter that it's Yorkville. Or, actually, it's *because* it's Yorkville. You get people doing drugs in the toilets, trying to walk off with your liquor, your sound system, your float, all kinda stuff. One time I find one of my tables in the middle of Cumberland Avenue, I tell no lie, Inspector, the tablecloth and menu card still right there on it, right in the middle of the damn road. So I keep the place locked up. No messing."

"And you're sure that yesterday nobody got in who wasn't supposed to be in?"

"I just told you, man. No. N-O."

"We have information, from a woman we interviewed last

night, that she was in here well before opening time. A Ms. Ravenscroft, her name is."

"Oh, yeah. Okay, then, now you mention it, yeah, I, myself, let that girl in. That whatshername . . . Kitten, she calls herself, I don't know nothing about no Ravenscross or whatever. She been hanging around the place for all of three days, day and night, looking sad and all by herself, Billy's not said boo to the poor child, put her out of her misery. So, yeah, okay, I took pity on her. That's all. 'No sense hanging around out here with a face like that, driving away my custom,' I says to her. 'Come on in, girl, and take a load off.' I mean, she was bad for business hanging around my entrance with a face like Judgment Day, man. At least she in here where I can watch what she's doing, dig? Calls herself Kitten, but she hang around my place like this mangy old black cat Briefs brought into here. Brung me nothin' but bad luck, you ask me."

"What time would that have been, sir — that you let Ms. Ravenscroft in?"

"I don't know. Four-thirty, maybe closer to five. And I don't know she was any Whatall Ravingscrop."

"So would she have been around when Billy came in to warm up or practise?"

"Yes, sir. I give her a drink, a raspberry vodka, she wanted, and she went and sat over at a table on the south wall, all by herself, where she parked herself on the two nights before that, too, the whole nights, nursing one, maybe two little drinks. But, like I say, she's a quiet girl. Got a nice, sad smile on her face. Don't bother nobody. Sits around writing in her book all the time, that's all, waiting for Billy, nursing a couple of flavoured vodkas. Not my cup of tea, but that's her business, know what I'm sayin'? She was really hepped up on seeing Billy, too, like I say, but that's not unusual. Lotsa people, women and men, wanted a piece of Billy Wonder. And I didn't think Billy would mind. Never had before. Seen him talk to her a couple times. Play the crowd, you know."

"And the doors were locked after you let the girl in?"

"Double-bolted, Inspector, up until official opening time. Tight as an alcoholic at the sunset end o' happy hour."

⁓ღ⁓

As the police investigation proceeds, His Lordship, Justice Theodore E. Mariner, passes almost as much time taking in the afternoon talk and advice shows as he spends in his own chambers. Most afternoons after court sittings find him at Jersey's bar, sipping an orange-cranberry cocktail, alcohol-free but its decorative cherry radioactively bright with Red Dye Number Whatever, craning his neck up at the television set as Oprah dispenses her Yankee blend of spiritual materialism, and Dr. Phil talks to the Other Woman about Why She Can't Stop Serial Homewrecking. "Profoundly superficial," His Lordship pronounces, smiling vaguely in the blue light. "Oprah's the plump, giving Every-mommy, Earth Mother, dig, and Dr. Phil's the powerful Uberdaddy, Sky Father, parenting an infantile culture that always needs to be told what to do. Or *wants* to be told, so that it doesn't have to take the responsibility. Plagues the justice system, of course. I see it everyday from the bench." Then, right on cue, here comes Hell's grandma (I guess), the underworld's Judge Judy, sneering and bullying her way through yet another case of a world-weary mother suing her welfare-bum son for absconding with the bail bond cash that Mom borrowed from her alcoholic ex-husband to put up for sonny-boy, who inevitably is charged with domestic violence on his girlfriend, with whom he's had two kids apprehended by Family Services. (Even if I try not to watch, you can hear the din throughout the decaying old building.) The producers pay Judge Judy millions to adjudicate, but His Lordship calls it shooting fish in a barrel. Still, he admits that her show taps into the inherent human drama of the courtroom ("Aristotelian," he lectures his fellow barflies, "in its respect for the tragic unities"), and he howls when Jersey switches off the set and shoos him out of the bar.

"Hey, it's research, man," Justice Mariner objects. "I'm keeping in touch — keeping grounded, as Oprah puts it — now that I've got the chance. Finding out how the popular mind really sees the administration of justice, how the public views the issues we deal with every day, you know? That kid was out on bail and breached his conditions, see?"

"Yeah, and on the show before it," Jersey says, pausing to pucker his lips and aim his shot, "married mens was running around with girls with nothing to lose. Geezers that should know better than thinking with their private parts. Dating their secretaries, picking up girls in nightclubs. Ring any bells, Briefs?"

The judge rolls his eyes. "Running around? I'm here, ain't I?" Day by day he seems to fall more deeply into the vernacular of the streets. He be bad, His Lordship. Real bad, in Jersey's opinion. "How can I be running around if I'm sitting at your bar, right in your face?"

"Tell you the truth, you got a point. You in my face. You out there fooling around with your law clerk, least you wouldn't be scuffing up my upholstery all day, propping up my bar and getting yourself a ulcerated intestines on them raggedy-acid fruit juices. Wearing out my remote and running up my 'lectricity bill on top of it. Shit."

"Shit," Justice Mariner responds, a word I have never heard pass his lips heretofore. He stands, elaborately pushing himself away from the bar.

"All I know is, you keep this up, I won't have a single regular left in my place."

"Oh, nice, Jers. Keep what up, exactly?"

"Professor lessons on the great Aristo-teetotalin' drama of the friggin' courtroom trial. Just what we need on top of your life story all afternoon. *Pissing and Moaning* by His Honour, Judge Briefs What Got His Sorry White Ass Kicked Out of His Own Damn Marriage Bed. Subtitle, *How Sad Be My Wussy Ol' Forest Hill Behind*. Shit, Briefs. Cry me a river. What you doin' to yourself, man, a smart, rich old boy like you? Why you wasting all your time in this sad old piss-ant bar, man?"

A few days later (just long enough to permit him to say it was in his own good time), His Lordship takes Jersey's tough love (as Oprah and Dr. Phil inevitably would have called it) to heart. He gets out his old University of Toronto cross-country singlet (the one that says 7T3 on the back, marking the year he graduated with a B.A. in philosophy) and starts running up to the campus, around Victoria College and through Queen's Park. He manages to get Jersey out with him on subsequent occasions (after the old impresario graciously responds to each and every invitation with, "If it'll get your lazy behind out o' my business, I guess I got to, don't I?") along with, on one ill-fated occasion, Des Cheshire.

Hacking up a quarter century of nicotine and bile, wearing basketball high-tops, brown dress socks, and a pair of swimming trunks borrowed from Jersey (gear three sizes too big for his nonexistent hind end and stick legs), Des is obliged to stop just after Bloor Street — after about one-and-a-half blocks, in other words — and stagger back coughing and spitting to the Alley.

As the judge and Jersey return from such a run one afternoon, I hear Justice Mariner ask, "You ever hear what happened to Donna, Jers?"

"Donna?" Jersey raises his T-shirt to wipe the sweat with it from his face. "Don't know no Donna, Briefs. If I went off home with her on some former occasion you might be referring to, I especially don't know her."

For the record, these forty-some years Jersey has been "scrappily married," as Des Cheshire describes it, to Nellie Doucette, who, though retired from the Ministry of Community and Social Services after thirty-five years there as a clerk, has not made a personal appearance at the Alley for a couple of decades. There is little doubt that Jersey has been scrupulously faithful to her, never mind the rumour, which Jersey refuses to confirm or deny, that when he proposed marriage, Nellie replied, "Now what would we want to go and do that for?" Jersey allegedly responded, "Well, you got the same name as Monk's wife, don't you?" On the strength of this romantic colloquy, he and Nellie booked their wedding reception at Birdland, it was said, where Thelonius Monk himself played his famous "Crepuscule with Nellie" as the newlyweds took over the dance floor, still eyeing each other warily.

"Yes you do so know her, and you liked her, too. She was my old girlfriend, man. Remember? Donna Nippelman. She used to wait tables for you sometimes. I brought her in when you couldn't get replacement staff."

"You mean the one that bought you them underpants with the weigh-scales on 'em, like at the fish market?"

"Yeah, the scales of justice. Donna Nippelman."

"Briefs," Jersey spits into the old tub sink in the Alley's kitchen, "that was like thirty years ago, man. How'm I supposed to know where she's at, Donna Perky-Bosoms or whatever she is, man? Shit. You livin' in the past, man."

"I'm thinking about looking her up."

"Oh, Lord," Jersey says, shaking his head, snuffling and sweating. "This is where I get off, man. You be running backwards, Mr. Justice Briefs. Beep, beep, beep, beep, look out! Pretty soon your skinny behind gonna hit the wall and hit it hard. Beep, beep, beep. Look out, folks! Here come Mr. Justice Briefs full speed, in reverse. You don't believe me, you just see for yourself, Briefs. Through that rearview mirror you can't take your eyes off of. You goin' backwards, and straight over some kinda damn cliff. I can see it clear as day. Yes I surely can."

～☙～

"Were there any particular tensions in the group itself? The quartet, I mean." The interlocutor is another old acquaintance, Detective Sergeant Siobhan Donovan of the Metropolitan Toronto Police Service, 52 Division. She has squeezed into Jersey's storeroom office along with Staff Inspector Gullion, who sits in Jersey's rickety old maple chair, a kitchen relic that probably came from a rummage sale or somebody's garbage along with the lame card table the old dyspeptic uses as his desk. To Gullion's left, Sergeant Donovan leans against a stack of boxes, her arms folded and her shiny black boots crossed as I look down on her neatly combed scalp from the top box — another Humpty Dumpty potato chip carton, as it happens — a few feet above. Donovan and I first met when she was crime scene leader in what turned out to be *The Queen against Slovenskaya* back at Osgoode Hall. She is easily as pretty as Joy Almundy, but goes for the natural look, which suits her genuinely honey-blonde hair (naturally streaked a little with reddish-brown strands), her clear, light skin, and her high Celtic cheekbones. Most notably unlike Joy Almundy, the only aroma wafting from Sergeant Donovan is the perfumed soap and powder from her morning shower. Where something seems to be missing from Almundy, the police officer is all woman, including her backbone. She holds Terry Denver's gaze with her gimlet brown eyes, and he blinks first. As she has pointed out to him, his drumsticks were around Billy Wonder's neck on the night in question.

"Tensions in the group?" Denver shrugs. "Nothing out of the ordinary."

"And what was ordinary?" Inspector Gullion asks.

"Well," Denver shrugs again, "I guess it's no secret that Des has never been happy with his contract."

"Oh, yeah? Why is he unhappy about it?" Sergeant Donovan moves back in.

Denver shrugs yet again. He is a short, wiry man with a thin, heavily-lined face and beak-like nose — a hatchet-face, as some Has-beings call it. Although he must be about fifty years old, he has the look of a young rascal, a street kid out of *Great Expectations*, if not exactly the Artful Dodger. His fingers are unnaturally long for his size, his hands strong from years at the battery. And he is a reluctant talker, at least at first. "Well, you know, Billy had him exclusive. He can't gig with any other piano players, for one thing. Or he couldn't. I suppose now he's free to do what he wants." Leaning on his knees as he sits in front of the card table, Denver looks at the dirty old storeroom floor, smirking to himself but so the rest of us can see.

"Was that a big issue between them?"

"Sometimes. Billy accused Des of violating the spirit of the thing by gigging with guitarists, you know, and one time with Lionel Hampton — on the vibes, years ago. Billy said it was the same diff. Des said vibes and guitar ain't a piano. Billy said same diff. And on and on like that. I say banana, you say tomato."

"But Des stayed with the group."

"Yeah. Billy was good at getting the work, even in shitty times for jazz, which is most of the time, although things have improved a little lately. Spiked. But generally most guys would kill to be in Billy's bands. In that sense, Des isn't too proud. He fancies himself an intellectual. Business is beneath him and all that. And he has this sort of depressive, pseudo-Beatnik side, you know. Mr. Angst. Keeps himself to himself a lot of the time, 'specially when we're travelling. So Billy did the legwork for him, as he did for all of us, naturally. And somehow Mr. Intellectual doesn't exactly mind business like that. Somebody else doing it for him." Denver allows himself a more frank sneer, then cracks a genuine smile, looking up at the detectives. "Mind you, the agreement also said that Billy got seventy-five per cent of Des's royalties on whatever he composed while he was under contract with Billy. Pretty one-sided, I guess."

"And was *that* a big issue?" Inspector Gullion asks.

"Well, when Des's 'Big Band Theory' became a hit, it was sort of an issue, I guess. And ever since, of course. But even Des admits that without Billy the public never would've heard the tune. I mean, Billy's popularity helped showcase it, understand. As it is, most folks outside the business think Billy wrote it."

"He didn't?" Sergeant Donovan flashes a high-beam, toothy smile at the drummer. It works, too. Denver relaxes his shoulders and sits up straight, smiling back.

"No, ma'am," he says. "But that stuff didn't get in the way, in particular. I mean, they've been together for twenty years or so, Billy and Des. They even shared girlfriends. Just like Tweedledum and Tweedledee, I guess. Love and hate all mixed up, all in the family, you know? The Moonshine Boys, Des calls himself and Billy. Called Billy, I guess. Like I say, he's a real wit."

"Moonshine? Because they drink?"

"Well, not exactly. It's more of a pun on *The Sunshine Boys*, the play, you know, about the bickering comedy duo? And of course jazz musicians are creatures of the night."

"You say they shared girlfriends. Did that include Ms. Almundy?"

"She'd dated both of them, yeah. But when she was with Billy, they had some real dust-ups as a couple, and it wasn't completely in private. I mean, Joy's not exactly your submissive one-man woman." Denver rolls his eyes and laughs. "She can be a regular hell-cat. But that stuff bounced off Billy, mostly, unless you pushed him or he was especially stressed out. Des says Billy always figured Joy was sleeping with him — with Billy — just to get the gigs. You couldn't put much past Billy, that's for sure. And the jungle drums said Joy was sleeping with Tommy Profitt at the same time." Denver shrugs and smiles. "I know Billy didn't have much use for Joy as a singer after they broke up. But she hangs around all the same, on the off-chance, I guess. She's sort of a lost soul, really, although she hides it desperately well under that glamour-puss diva act of hers."

"Were she and Billy still talking?"

Denver shrugs again. "Sure. Why not?"

"What about you? How long have you been with the quartet?"

Denver looks up, thinking, and spots Yours Earwiggingly near the ceiling, on the dusty potato chip box. He laughs and points at me. "We've got a snoop."

Startled, the cops look up at me. Reflexively, Gullion touches his belt, near the holster for his service revolver. *Don't shoot, boss!* "Kitty, kitty," Donovan calls, as I blink, lick my lips, and yawn. Then I pretend to go to sleep, as though I couldn't care less.

"How long have I been with Billy?" Denver picks up the thread, scrunching his nose and gazing at me still, as though I had the answer. "I'd say nearly four years now." As he seems about to add something, the detectives keep studiously mum. "Also, I guess I might as well just say it, because it's going to come up eventually. It's another non-secret that there's no love lost between me and Des. It's nothing serious. We just have different personalities."

"How do you mean?" Donovan asks.

"Well, again, I just think he's a bit of a snob, and I'm only trying to keep the customers happy, is what it comes down to, I guess. Play the gig, collect my pay. He has this attitude that if it's popular, it must be stupid. To me, if the average person likes it, it pays the bills, you know? It keeps you going. Billy had sort of the middle view, so it worked, see? Des pretends that he only keeps playing 'Theory' because Billy insists. Insisted." Denver shakes his head a̱ d looks at the floor again. "Jesus, I can't believe he's gone. It's weird, you know? Just like that. No more Bill." He shakes his head again. "Anyway, jazz started out as popular music, didn't it? Dance music, like rock 'n' roll. Des, he sees it like it's chamber music or even symphonic, and Thelonius Monk's the new Mozart. We just don't agree on that. It's bullshit. The only reason jazz struggles is that players like him deny its popular dance roots."

As Denver describes his populist view contrasted with Des Cheshire's elitist stance, I recall the quartet's opening night at the Alley, just before I fled for quieter territory upstairs. The band was playing what Wonder had introduced as "our abbreviated version of *Forest Flower* by Charles Lloyd." In mid-tune, as Denver began his extended solo, Des capped and racked his horn, then went to a table off to the side of the stage where he ostentatiously began reading a book in the afterglow of the stage lights.

"It's *War and Peace*," Joy Almundy said, giggling, nodding Des's way.

"What is?" Norman Clapham, Almundy's jumpy boyfriend, asked, looking worried that hostilities might have broken out in his vicinity.

Almundy clicked her tongue in disgust. "The *book*, nimrod. The *book* Des is reading over there." She nudged him really hard with her elbow, and he looked appropriately chastised until she kissed his cheek.

"When we were in Columbus last week," Billy's local rep, Morgan Denny, added, laughing, "it was Kafka's short stories. He claims he read all of 'The Hunger Artist' during a single drum solo by Terry."

Sure enough, Denver riffed off the Latin feel of the tune for several minutes, in a very flashy solo somewhat reminiscent of Buddy Rich or Gene Krupa by way of Carlos Santana. As Whitehead and Billy came back in and Denver finished off to loud cheers from the semi-drunken crowd — a few people even stood as they applauded and whooped — Des crammed the paperback Tolstoy into his jacket pocket, leapt back onstage, and re-hitched his horn to his neck strap. And he came in right on cue.

"For Des, popular equals dumb," Denver tells the detectives. "Unsophisticated."

"So have you talked to him about this difference of opinion?" Gullion asks.

Denver screws up his face and shakes his head. "Not lately. It isn't worth the trouble. He's always got some smart-ass answer, so it's just easier not to say anything. That way, we get along just fine. I mean, we're in each other's laps eleven months out of the year, day and night, you know? No matter what. Planes, trains, buses, hotels. We can't afford to be at each other's throats." Realizing that his metaphor hits a sour note in the circumstances, Denver adds, "It's a matter of staying professional, see, biting your tongue but not so hard you can't play? We work okay together, besides those few distractions. If it ever got worse, I'd speak to him. I mean, if it interfered with the job."

"I would think so." Sergeant. Donovan nods. "Did you ever speak to Billy about it, though?"

Denver rolls his eyes. "Every goddamn day." Suddenly he looks uncomfortable again. "Look, I don't mean to make things difficult for Des or anything. As I say, he's a good player and all that. But I think Billy was scared of him. He put up with his bullshit because he was afraid Des would walk, and take the group's respectability with him."

"But don't band leaders always put up with all kinds of stuff for the same reason?" Gullion asked. "Dope, drinking, showing up late? Because that's part of the music scene or whatever?"

"Yeah, they have to put up with that malarkey, which is exactly why Des can't be bothered to start his own outfit."

"But he never gave Wonder that kind of grief?"

"No. He'll have a tipple now and then, but he's certainly no junkie. He's an Irish whiskey man, actually. But he likes to say he's addicted to only one mind-altering substance: women. And it's true; chasing skirt is his preferred vice. Still, yeah, he does his job, I'll give him that. He shows up and he plays to kill. He's very professional." Denver swallows, glances more frankly at Gullion, and half-shrugs. "And like I say, you should know that it wasn't really bad blood between them, as far as I'm aware. I mean, I want to be fair, here, guys. You might know that Des even wrote a tune for Billy a few year's back, a sort of tribute, you know? We play it all the time — 'I Get a Schtick Out of You.' 'Schtick,' we call it, for short. It's on the *S'WONDERful* album, from before I was with the band."

Apparently Billy was Cheshire's muse on more than one occasion, depending on his mood. The dark lady of his sonnets, as it were.

"And you? Are you a model employee?"

Denver purses his lips and shakes his head. "No one ever accused me of that. Occasionally I've had one too many the night before a gig. Just like everyone else — except Saint Des, I guess. I'm late to work sometimes. Rehearsals. Never gigs." The room goes quiet for several moments, until Terry Denver looks up again at the resident feline near the ceiling and says: "I mean, I really don't want to sound like a crybaby or a snitch here, folks. No kidding. I suppose they said the same about Milton Berle or Louis B. Mayer. Des is a funny guy. But it's not all that funny when you have to live with him. You know what I mean? Catch this, for instance. You know what's the first thing Des says after we find out Billy's really dead?" He glances from one to the other of the detectives. "He says, and I kid you not, Des says, 'Great. I guess that means we'll have to call our next CD, *Billy Wonder: Dead at the Chicken Alley!*'"

∾ᨓ∾

Jersey was right, of course. This jaunty renaissance of youth thing is starting to get out of hand. Now His Lordship is looking at a career change. As a piano man, no less.

"Profitt's not shown up, man," Jersey complains. "Left me high and frickin' dry again. Plain ol' vamoosed. Spooked, I guess."

"Unless he actually did it. The murder, I mean."

Jersey shakes his head. "Don't have the balls for it. Left me holdin' 'em instead, looks like."

"Well, you've got Joy Whatshername, don't you? Al. . . ." Justice Mariner looks inquisitively at his old employer.

"Almundy."

"Almundy." The judge nods, as if he'd known the singer personally for years.

"And exactly who's going to accompany her, Briefs? Any bright ideas on that?"

"Well, my chops aren't really up, I guess, but they'll run to a couple of tunes with her. I can still play stuff like 'Ain't Misbe-havin'' and maybe 'Blue Skies' or something." His Lordship mulls for a few seconds. "You don't really forget those old standards, do you, Jers? 'Honeysuckle Rose.'"

"Oh, great, bud. All the hits of two centuries ago."

"'The Best Is Yet to Come.'"

"No it ain't. You might be pretty good setting on your butt up on some bench over at the courthouse, but you got no best on the piano bench, Briefs."

"'Don't Get Around Much Any More.'"

"Exactly what I been trying to tell you, sitting on your fanny at the bar all day. Tell you what, then. Why don't we just try this: 'Do Nothin' 'Til You Hear From Me.'"

"Man, there's no helping some people. You know, Jers, you've become one incredible miseryguts. A grumpy old granny. I mean, I'm offering you a hand, here. It's better than no talent at all, isn't it?"

"If it actually went beyond no talent, yeah."

Taking a page from Jersey's own fake book, Justice Mariner just eyeballs the aged impresario.

"Well, I suppose Joy could accompany herself on her guitar on a couple other tunes." Jersey looks a little apologetic, for Jersey. "And maybe she can do a couple with just Terry and Bones. You know, just the rhythm section. But then what I'm gonna do, Briefs, 'specially after half my place empties out two tunes into your frickin' set o' Golden Mouldies?"

The two old friends sit at the bar looking opposite ways toward the ceiling for a few seconds. Then Justice Mariner slaps Jersey's back. "I guess we'll just have to play some more and drive the rest of them out."

Jersey rolls his eyes and shakes his head. "You wouldn't be getting big ideas about yourself, now, would you, Briefs? One, this ain't the fifties no more. Two, maybe you're thinkin' like suddenly you free as a bird, a swingin' single and all that, Mrs. Your Lordship throw'd you out. But you ain't no kid no more, kid. Playin' like you the new old Dave Brubeck. Looking up your girlfriends from your little black book, when the damn book's older than both your growed-up daughters. One of them my own little god-daughter, on top of it. Got twice the sense of her frickin' daddy." That would be the oldest, Catherine, the Bay Street corporate lawyer. "You swing the wrong way, Briefs, you be puttin' your back out for a month. Mm-hmm. And that chiropractor, he costs some serious money. Mm-hmm."

"I can recall the tunes, Jers. I'm a judge, remember? I'm used to remembering bankers' boxes of complicated stuff, and then spilling it all back out — giving judgments and jury charges and all that. It's my job, man. All motor memory. Automatic pilot."

"You think my customers come in here by compulsory draft or something? They a jury now, for your musical misdemeanours?"

"Well, doesn't it amount to the same deal? They sit in judgment of you every night — of your performers, your bar staff, your food, your beer, the Alley itself, no?"

Jersey thinks about it briefly then shrugs. "Yeah, okay, then. Beggars can't be Florence Ziegfield, I guess. But, Briefs."

"Yeah, Jers."

"You knock 'em on their ass, else I knock you on yours. And you know I will."

"Hey, I know you love us, man. Else why'd you let us stay with you?"

"'Cause I'm outta my tiny frickin' mind, that's why." Jersey hoists his aged behind off the stool and lopes painfully around the bar, grumbling on, his boombox voice fading as he shuffles toward his storeroom office. "Getting involved in other folks' domestic situations. Outta my teeny tiny frick-frackin' little mind. Pickin' up ever'body's waifs and strays. Shee-it, mama. Shee-frickin'-it . . ."

CHAPTER 4

Ain't Misbehavin'

"Oy, Miss! 'Scuse me, Miss. Whaddaya think you're doing there?"

Much vexed, a pudgy young constable comes huffing up to Joy Almundy, who has slipped under the yellow police tape around the Chicken Alley's stage and picked up a battered old poster-board guitar case. It has a sticker on it that says, "Don't tell me what kind of day to have."

Almundy gives the constable a dismissive glance and tells him, "I don't think anything, officer. I've gone straight into doing. And it's nothing you have to worry about, I can assure you." She looks him up and down and then begins to walk away with the case.

The constable scoots after her, sideways. "I'm afraid you'll have to put that back just where you found it, and then stay behind the tape, please." He is sweating and has to stop himself from wringing his hands. "And now we'll have to have your finger-prints, besides."

Almundy stops and laughs loudly. "They would have been all over this thing anyway, sonny-boy. It's my guitar, for Christ's sake." She smiles coldly at the poor kid, staring at him hard with her gold-flecked green eyes until he blushes. "And you already got my dabs last night. Crikey, where'd you get your training, the Keystone Cops Matchbook Academy?"

The kid probably never heard the word "dabs" in his life. Softly, looking off to the side, he says, "I'm really sorry, miss, but until we're finished, it's ours. It's crime scene evidence. We'll do our best to get it back to you in good condition."

"That would be nice, considering it's a piece of shit now."

"Problem?" It's Detective Sergeant Donovan, just out of her interview with Terry Denver.

"Not for me," Almundy sneers. "I've just come for my piece of shit." She gestures with the guitar case.

"That's yours, is it?"

The singer sighs and rolls her eyes. "No, I just thought I'd steal somebody else's crappy old axe, seeing how the joint's lousy with cops and I've got nowhere to sleep tonight."

"Why was it on the bandstand?"

Almundy puts the instrument on the floor and makes an extravagant show of being patient. "Bones — Jimmy Whitehead, Billy's bass player — Bones and I were just messing around yesterday afternoon. Jamming. As you might have noticed, or maybe you didn't, I sometimes sing with the band. So I was hoping to sit in last night. Then that idiot Billy goes and gets himself snuffed." She smiles and flutters her lashes at her younger, naturally blonder, and considerably less pretentious interlocutor. "As you might have heard?"

The police sergeant purses her lips as Joyless retrieves her guitar case. "Break any strings, Ms. Almundy?"

Joyless shakes her head in puzzled disgust. "No." She puts a hand on her hip, and Donovan holds her gaze. "But just to put your mind at rest, I have a new package, a full set, anyway, in here." She waggles the case.

"Actually, you don't," Sergeant Donovan says, smiling and arching her brows. "The package has been opened, and the low E string is missing."

∽᳁∼

"Jersey thinks I'm going through male menopause. Or 'mental-pause,' as he calls it."

Running his finger around the lip of his glass of Bushmills, Des Cheshire smiles dreamily. "Hey, man, go for it. Never mind James Bond. You only live *once*. There's no second chances. Which is why I take them whenever possible. If you get my drift. Enjoy your second childhood, and your third."

Justice Mariner shakes his head skeptically, pulling on the unlit cigarette in his mouth as he, Cheshire, and Norman Clapham sit at Jersey's bar. "Well, but, you know, we're not twenty-three years old any more, Donna and I. Especially I, if you get *my* drift."

"Hey, age has nothing to do with it. Follow your Muse, man."

"Isn't that doomed to failure, though," Clapham pedantically asks, "by definition? You can't conquer the Muse, right, or it's game over? Nothing left to keep you going. It's like capturing the Sirens. They eat you up. Who's predator, who's prey?"

"The chase *is* the point, homes." Cheshire picks up his drink and salutes Clapham with it. "We're always both predator *and* prey, and there's always a new ideal to go after. You bag a trophy, doesn't mean you stop the hunt. To keep going, the soul needs new nourishment. Manifest destiny and all that. You lose some, you win some more. *C'est*, literally, *la vie*."

"You know, I just don't buy that," Clapham shakes his head. "That 'what doesn't kill me makes me stronger' business. I think failure just wears you out. Uses you up faster than normal. I think you need to actually kill what weakens you, for your own good, you know? Let it go, move on, like they say on *Dr. Phil*."

The judge stares at the bar top pretending not to know what Clapham is talking about.

Des laughs. "Tommy's got a routine about this, you know. The whole chasing the Muse thing — chasing some impossible love-dream. Sounds trite, but it's actually one of his best bits." He drags on his smoke and lets it dangle on his lower lip. "Which isn't saying much, mind you."

It was the centrepiece to a larger bit, in fact, about the abject failure of Profitt's love life, the stock-in-trade for the stand-up comic. *When I was in college,* he would say, *they called the ballplayer Reggie Jackson "Mr. October." This was because he always hit a lot of homeruns, scored really big, in the playoff games and the World Series in the fall. Mr. October. Myself, I never saw much action any time of the year. They used to call me Mr. February 29th. Mr. Leap Year.* He would segue from there into his unrequited love for his alleged grade school sweetheart, Karen Gillis. *Yes, folks, she was a lovely little thing,* he would exclaim, his face muscles slackening with pretend nostalgia, *little Karen Gillis. Elfin, shy, a study in browns — a quiet brunette with mocha skin and big chestnut eyes, like a little puppy's. But she didn't follow me around at all, not even to pull on my trouser legs with her teeth. She hardly knew I existed.*

I lost track of little Karen after grade school, until one day, as if fate had thrown us together like Romeo and Juliet, we met again at a coffee shop where I was writing the Great American Novel. Or maybe it was just this sorry-ass bit I'm doing here now. Anyway, we went back to my writer's garret — my old room in my parents' basement in the suburbs. It's all pretty much a blur now, but I remember that in the middle of the night we got out of bed — or up off the old mattress I'd rescued from the neighbour's garbage — and Karen stood at my side. My Muse, Karen Gillis, conquered at last, whispering to me as I sat at my computer, taking down her words.

When I woke up the next morning there was no sign of my brown-eyed girl. I hurried anxiously over to my computer for some memento of my night of passion with my Muse, something to prove to me that it hadn't all been just some wet dream. Something for literature and posterity. I switched on the monitor, and, sure enough, I found a couplet:

> *"Unable to create document or folder;*
> *Failure computes as a permanent error."*

"So if I look Donna Nippelman up, you think I'll just get an error message?" With a hangdog half-smile, His Lordship glances from Cheshire to Clapham and back to Cheshire again.

"We were discussing Victorian literature the other night, Judge," Clapham responds. "Have you ever read any William Butler Yeats?"

"Just that thing about the swan bonking the woman." He squints at Clapham, as if the cigarette were really lit and its smoke stinging his eyes. Cool dude. *(Yeah, right.)*

"*Leda and the Swan*," Clapham annotates. "The swan is actually the Greek god Zeus in disguise. But I'm thinking of Yeats's poem *The Tower*. It commemorates the actual place where he wrote, night after night, trying to reach the Muse. 'Does the imagination dwell the most,' he asks, 'upon a woman won or woman lost?' He concludes that pining for the woman lost, the one that got away, that's what poets do. Literally, they moon — their art eclipses 'the prosaic light of day' and makes moonlit poetry. They become sort of lucid lunatics. So domesticating the Muse, reaching and conquering the Moon Goddess, 'is an achievement the Tower never reaches,' Yeats says. Conquest kills art."

"Which maybe explains why lunar astronauts are exclusively scientists and not poets or musicians," Cheshire notes, raising his glass again.

The judge laughs and says to Cheshire, "He's very big on Victorian literature, is our Norman." Then he turns seriously to Clapham. "But the point is, Norman, the poet keeps trying for the Muse, even if he can never really catch her without destroying himself. The alternative is what? Stasis; death, anyway."

"Well, but that's my point. Either way, all poor old Yeats got out of it was frustrated. He might have lived longer, actually, without all that striving and pining and misery over that unresponsive actress, what was her name? — Maude Gonne, his unrequiting love. Prick-teaser, more like."

Cheshire widens his eyes at Clapham's fervour, then toasts his companions again with the last of his Irish whiskey. "Ah, but it's the creative force, man. The juice that keeps our motors revving. You see it in the clubs night after night. You have to keep offering your creative potential in the marketplace. It's nature's way. Just ask Ted's little ol' tomcat."

"I thought that, too." Clapham deliberately fixes each of his companions with a brief stare, one after the other, the smile fading from his face. "But not any more. Reaching beyond your grasp. It just wears you out."

∽✲∽

The same old unlit fag dangling from his lips, Ted Mariner hunches over Jersey's piano, a picture of relaxed concentration. Shadowy in the gloaming on stage, you can see young Briefs Mariner, the laconic law student and Chicken Alley dogsbody of thirty years earlier. His busboy's cheeks now sallow and a little creased, his gaze dimmed a little by the grief he has seen as a lawyer and a judge — deepened by genuine angst, as opposed to the *poseur's* variety he sometimes affected in his youth — he remains handsome and lanky, his trim frame rocking a little with the changes to "Good Morning Heartache." "It's slow and conventionally melodic, so I can keep up with you." Thus has he pleaded his case before a skeptical Joy Almundy, who now sings to the judge's tasteful, understated accompaniment. And for a Hasbeing of her unfortunate disposition and pallid skin colour, she makes not a bad job of it.

Good morning, Heartache. Sit down.

There is scattered but sincere applause. Then with help from Tommy Whitehead on bass, Joy picks up the pace with the jokey jazz-rap, "My Analyst Told Me." *My analyst told me / that I was right out of my head. . . .* With a nod to popular culture, she performs the tune hip-hop style, with a heavily accented beat. His eyes on the floor, Briefs Mariner leaves the stage, waves goodnight to Jersey without glancing toward the bar, and climbs the old stairs to bed, feeling dizzy and lost as the years descend to meet him.

❧

"He was garrotted, then?" Des Cheshire sits at his favourite Alley table, behind stage right, against the Yorkville Avenue wall. He is in his shirtsleeves, never mind that there is no insulation against the frigid winter air behind the cracked plaster. A chain smoker, he accidentally drops ash into his coffee — which anyway has long since gone cold — and all over his loosely knotted orange tie with the blue stripes. He seems to wear it with everything, no matter the colour contrast. Across from him sit Detectives Donovan and Yastremski. "Strangled with piano wire?"

"What makes you say that?" Yastremski asks, squinting against Cheshire's bylaw-breaching smoke.

"Come on. I was standing right there. It was wound around his neck, for Chrissake."

"Then you must know," Donovan cuts in, "that the wire wasn't piano wire."

Cheshire makes a wry face. "I didn't exactly get down on the floor with him for a better look at his fashion accessories."

"You would have needed to get down on the floor to recognize a guitar string?"

"Ah, yes, on second thought, I know that one," Cheshire says, pulling at one of his suspenders. "'Out of Air on the G String.'"

"It was an E string, actually," Yastremski informs the witness, after no one laughs. "The thickest one, wound with brass. And if you think it's funny, you should see what it did to your boss's windpipe."

"Why did you use the term 'garrotted'?" Donovan asks.

"Because when the lights came up I was certainly close enough to see the drumsticks."

"Meaning . . . ?"

"Well, that's how a garrotte works, right? You use a stick or something to twist the wire tighter. It's easier than using your own brute strength." Cheshire laughs. "That's what separates us from the animals, isn't it? Tools?"

"You really find it amusing?" Yastremski asks.

"That we're supposed to be a higher life form than this chubby little cat here, for instance?" Cheshire rubs at my left ear. "You betcha. I think it's a real hoot."

"How do you know about the way garrotting works?" Donovan gets the witness back to the *modus operandi*.

Cheshire shrugs as his smile dims and his face goes contemplative. "I don't know. I must've read about it somewhere. It was a method of execution in Spain. And Portugal, too, I believe. Capital punishment. We've played in both countries. Maybe I saw something about it in a museum. That's what I do, if there's time. I go to the museums, galleries, book shops, historical sites. I look around the towns. If the opportunity knocks and all that. The other guys get up at two in the afternoon, then go sit in the dark and get plastered until it's time to work. Then they get plastered some more, fall into bed at dawn, and start all over again the next afternoon. They never see daylight. I don't call that living, unless you're a mushroom."

"You mean when you travelled with Billy Wonder?" Yastremski remains poker-faced.

"That's right."

"You're not really friendly with the rest of band?"

Cheshire shrugs again. "Can you say you're really friendly with your family? But you still have Christmas dinner with them, don't you?"

"You've been under contract with Wonder for a long time."

Cheshire lights another cigarette. "Since Adam were a lad, I believe the expression goes."

"And it's more or less exclusive?"

"More or less." Cheshire nods, then crinkles his nose. "Billy certainly had a right of first refusal, and he was very good at saying no."

"You don't sound very happy about the relationship."

"I hated it. It was like being stuck in a bad marriage. But then, I hate running the show and putting up with all the administrative bullshit more. As I say, Billy was really good at saying no. I'm shit at it. It was a marriage of convenience, and to that extent it worked."

"You've done very well with Billy," Detective Donovan says.

Cheshire nods. "Reasonably so, materially speaking."

"One of your songs was a hit on every radio station on the continent."

"It was a tune, not a song, detective — wordless. And it was a hit across the world."

"Well, there you go, then."

Cheshire takes a drag on his smoke and shakes his head. "Go where? What good is praise from people who can't tell a Michelangelo from a Michelob?" The detectives do not reply, so Cheshire adds, "You know, Schoenberg once said, 'If it is art, it is not for all, and if it is for all, it is not art.' I'm all for art, except I can't afford it."

"If you could afford it, chances are it wouldn't be for *you*," Detective Donovan says, and Cheshire looks at her with new respect.

"True enough. I'd probably be running a widget factory or

something. And living the high old life — country homes on three continents, private jets, starlets — courtesy of the minor share-holders and their pension funds."

"And all this touring and fame you find so hard to take, it's also brought you lots of attention from the ladies?" Yastremski asks, rather bitterly, it seems to me. "That hard to take, too?"

"Musicians often do all right in that department. Even poor and obscure ones, Detective. I've heard it's the same in the police department. Women like uniforms, the story goes, or is it those big sticks dangling at your thighs?"

"Couldn't say." Yastremski tries hard to look unfazed. "Then again, we don't date our buddies' girlfriends."

"Girlfriends. Which girlfriends do you mean?"

"Joy Almundy, for example?"

Cheshire laughs again and looks genuinely surprised. "That ballbreaker's somebody's girlfriend? I assure you, detective, she's purely a prick teaser. And in order to pull that game off success-fully, which she very much does, you can't belong to anybody in particular."

"You and Billy didn't date her?"

"I dated her. Billy dated her. Tommy dated her, for a night or two. The marine corps dated her."

"I don't know about the marine corps, but you don't really get along with Mr. Profitt, do you?" Donovan asks.

"Well, I'm funnier than he is. It drives him nuts. Then again, he's a fucking cokehead. Useless half the time. Burning out all his own wiring. Self-destructing. What a waste."

"And what about this Gianna Whatsername?" Yastremski says.

"Ravenscroft. Kitten Ravenscroft. She's no girlfriend, sir, not in a million years. She's at the front of the I-hate-Cheshire's-guts queue, just after Tommy Profitt. She's a stalker, and I told her as much, hounding Billy everywhere we go. I warned her off, told her there were laws against it. I thought I was doing her a favour, but of course she didn't take it that way. Joy had the same grief with her. Billy was too polite, protecting the fan base and all that, but we thought he was only hurting her, not to mention himself and the band — making it worse by not putting her out of her misery. Out of all our misery. So both Joy and I gave her the straight goods. Told her Billy thought she was crazy and a menace. Her response was that we were jealous." Cheshire throws up his hands, then gestures with his coffee cup at His Lordship, who sits at the bar with Oprah Winfrey, in her cathode ray thrall.

"Ravenscroft puts you in this club the day of the murder, at around five o'clock."

"Nope. I'd gone out to buy some new reeds and some fags. Then I mooched around the neighbourhood, got something to eat at the Four Seasons, and I didn't come back until just before we were supposed to go on. That's why none of us had a clue about what had happened. We went onto the bandstand in the dark, while Tommy was doing his schtick in front of the curtain. And before you ask, that wasn't unusual. Most nights Billy was the first one on the stand. I mean, it was his gig. His business. He was the leader, as you say. Mister Big."

"Then the witness is lying?"

Justice Mariner reheats Des Cheshire's coffee, cigarette ash and all. The musician shrugs and, squinting, pulls again on his smoke. "Mistaken, perhaps? The woman, Detective, swore she'd have Billy fire me, as if he would have listened to the nutbar. As if I wasn't the meal ticket for the whole band. This Kitten Ravenscroft, dig, threatened to kill *me*. She's one weird sister." Cheshire shakes his head, exhales a long jet of smoke out the side of his mouth, then adds: "My money's on her in this thing, kids, unless the butler did it."

Detective Sergeant Donovan ignores the lame joke. "So you're saying Billy was sitting at the piano dead and you had no idea or forewarning?"

"Forewarning? Look, some people think Billy's been dead for years. Musically, I'd have to agree."

"You really sound very bitter and sarcastic about your job, Mr. Cheshire," Sergeant Donovan says, sincerely vexed. I get the feeling she's got a thing for the famous musician and she's resisting the urge to make him prime suspect.

Perhaps sensing this, Cheshire smiles at her. "Bitter? My dear, we live in an era that takes superficiality to new depths."

Yes, likely he cadged that particular *bon mot* from the judge, but I resist finking him out to the cops.

Donovan smiles back as Yastremski snorts and says: "You're a real joker, aren't you Mr. Cheshire? A real wiseacre."

Jealousy, the green-eyed monster, Shakespeare calls it, in *Othello*, His Lordship informs me, as well as most of the litigants in his family law cases. It's everywhere.

Yastremski takes a card from his shirt pocket as he says, "Des or Desmond Cheshire, I am arresting you on a charge of first-degree murder in the death of Billy Wonder at the Chicken Alley nightclub and tavern on or about January thirteen of this year. You have the right . . ." Glancing at the card, Yastremski realizes that he holds it upside down. Donovan watches her colleague, biting her lower lip as Des smirks and takes the inevitable drag on his inevitable smoke. Yastremski turns the card so that he can inform Des according to formula of his right to retain and instruct counsel without delay, and that he is entitled to assistance in finding a lawyer. If he cannot afford counsel, legal aid will be made available.

That, of course, is where we really came into the picture, His Lordship and I, at least in our professional capacity. And Des's famous so-called dry humour doesn't help us much.

"You are not bound to say anything," Detective Donovan advises him, looking at the table, "but what you do say may be taken down by us and used against you."

"Your panties," Cheshire says, his smirk broadening, his eyebrows doing a Groucho Marx dance.

The detective collapses deliberately against her chair back, rolling her eyes and shaking her head.

"Well, what the hell do you expect?" Cheshire asks, in dead earnest now. "You charge me with murdering Billy Wonder and you think I'm going to take it seriously?"

CHAPTER 5

Just Squeeze Me

File no: *04081-MTPS/D52*
Willsay evidence of: *Gianna a/k/a "Jane" a/k/a "Kitten" Ravenscroft*
Interviewing officer: *S. Donovan, Det. Sgt., 52 Div.*
Interview date: *15/01/05*

The witness is 32 years old and ordinarily resident at 1415 South Chase St., Columbus, Ohio, USA. As attested and sworn to by her signature below, witnessed by the interviewing officer and the supervising officer on file no. 04081, the witness has provided the following evidence:

— I am ordinarily resident in Columbus, Ohio, USA, but I travel frequently in my work, in particular with the jazz ensemble, the Billy Wonder Quartet.
— I am a singer/songwriter, currently not in regular employment. Periodically I receive social assistance from the government of the State of Ohio.

— *The deceased victim, Billy Wonder, was in love with me and composed numerous compositions in my honour.*

— *I went everywhere Billy Wonder went. [*Handwritten interlineation: *We went everywhere together!!]*

— *There are those, including a psychiatrist who treated me [*handwritten interlineation: *who I consulted], and including certain members of the Billy Wonder entourage (Desmond Cheshire, Thomas Profitt), who attempted to interfere in my relationship with Billy Wonder, and who possibly are involved in his death. These persons persistently deny that Wonder feels anything for me "beyond mortal fear and loathing" (according to Des Cheshire, although I [*handwritten interlineation: strongly] *believe his opinion to be laughable as befits a class clown), or that Wonder has communicated with me through his music. This interference only drove me and Billy Wonder closer, making our love stronger.*

— *I do not suffer from any mental illness. I consulted the psychiatrist to deal with personal and career issues, and particularly to help me focus on my career as a singer/songwriter. The psychiatrist's name is Lawrence Hafner and he lives and works in Columbus, Ohio, USA.*

— *On the day of Billy Wonder's death, I was waiting for him at the front door of the Chicken Alley bar and grill in the Yorkville district of Toronto. The bar's owner, Jersey Doucette, told me that if I was going to "vagrant around my place," as Doucette put it, I might as well "loiter with the intent of running up a bar tab." Doucette invited me to wait for Wonder inside the bar. I sat at a table in the club section, drinking flavoured vodka and writing in my journal.*

— My journal is lost. It contained nothing of relevance to this investigation, only my random thoughts and jottings, my poems, my ideas for songs, drawings, etc. It contained strictly personal information.

— Someone was playing the piano in the Chicken Alley around five o'clock. I was certain it was Wonder, although I was unable to see him because the stage curtain was drawn. It sounded like Billy Wonder, but I did not wish to disturb his "warm-up" for the evening's performance.

— I saw Desmond Cheshire in the club shortly thereafter, behind the stage area. The stage is set forward of the back wall of the bar, such that there are tables behind it and all around it.

— I was absent from the table on three occasions, for short periods of time, but noticed nothing unusual until Billy Wonder's death was discovered when Doucette introduced the quartet to the audience. Those three occasions were as follows:

(1) Around five p.m., to assist Doucette I checked into a commotion made by the bar's cat, then I went to the washroom.

(2) I used the washroom again, shortly after seven o'clock p.m.

(3) Just before leaving the bar, at approximately 8:45 p.m., I used the washroom again.

— I neither saw nor heard a struggle, nor, previous to the discovery of the crime did I observe any sign that an assailant had attacked Billy Wonder.

I hereby swear or affirm that the above information was provided freely and voluntarily, without duress or promise of favour, and that it is true and accurate. I further understand that it is an offence under the *Criminal Code* to provide a statement to police that is untrue or misleading.

Signed, **Gianna Ravenscroft**.

Dated, this 15th *day of* January, 2005 *at* Toronto, Ontario, Canada.

Witnesses (signed): **M.S. Donovan, Det. Sgt.**
Peter M. Gullion, Det. Insp.

∼◦◦◦∼

Muses. Jealousy. Professional and personal rivalries. I proffer "Kitten" Ravenscroft's "willsay" — what she has told police and is expected to testify in court — because of course I never heard her interviewed. The questioning apparently took place at police headquarters on College Street, and we learned the details only when the Crown Attorney's office served its disclosure package a couple of weeks later.

You will note that in her statement Ravenscroft alludes to the so-called "bar's cat" causing a commotion. Well, Yours Personally can attest and affirm that Gianna a/k/a "Jane" a/k/a "Kitten" Ravenscroft never heard the actual feline commotion that night, because it came much later in the evening, so late that it was actually four hours into the next day. And talk about another blood-and-guts tale of woe . . .

By now you will have the impression that the Alley, and our domestic life in general, was in a considerable state of hormonal *frisson* if not outright cat-fighting. Unbeknownst (fortunately) to the witness Ravenscroft, things were no less heated in the real alley on the other side of the laneway which gives the Chicken Alley its name.

Strolling back to my digs above Jersey's club that night, I had come across Caboodle, a mature queen whose name must have been significantly more amusing when she was a kitten. Now, anyway, she was a plump, medium-hair calico with big splotches of earthy browns, orange, and black — clownish or fashionably colourful, depending on one's taste — on her otherwise bright white coat. Long since abandoned by a wealthy Rosedale family in the prolonged throes of what we barristers call matrimonial litigation, the voluptuous moggy now stood on her hind legs in the act of toppling one of the battered old beef tallow cans Jersey keeps as trash barrels. She was, in other words, raiding the larder for a midnight snack. Though frayed from my own night on the tiles of darkest Yorkville, I saluted the alley-wise feline fatale, who seemed to be in the full heat of estrus but, like many a female Has-being I'd observed in Jersey's club, she remained content to amuse herself by setting suitors against one another rather than by actually promoting the survival of the local population of strays. How better to tell who was the fittest mate, after all, than to get them brawling over you?

Inevitably, the environs were rich with contenders drunk on queenly pheromones and therefore willing to risk loss of life and limb on the off-chance of Caboodle's favours. *"Attention, donc!"* one suitor growled at that very moment. "That one, she is already spoken for, *là*, you old shyster." I at once recognized the wheezy, francophone rasp of Baudelaire, the aged gangbanger who these days considered himself the old lion of Uptown, having been chased north by the younger and fitter downtowner studs. And being of a more scholarly disposition, a lover and not a fighter, who was Yours Pacifically to argue with a punch-drunk street-fightin' tom, never mind that his only remaining eye had turned milky and the extant half of his ears, whittled down in past affrays, had gone brittle with dried pus? Mind you, I couldn't help noticing that the old soldier did not approach me, but sat shivering in the winter air against the back wall of the club, the wizzled socket of his missing eyeball turned away from the courtyard, to hide his weakness from dominant male interlopers.

Speaking of which, admiring his own swagger of youth, the party of the fourth part sauntered into a puddle of street light, sneering, "Yeah, and it's me who's doing all the pillow talk." It was that young downtowner, Tantôt, of course — pronounced "Tonto," as with the Lone Ranger's aboriginal sidekick, but from the French for "pretty soon," or, as Tantôt never tired of explaining, "When I bloody well get around to it." He was that sort of tom, a sleek, grey, amber-eyed tabby with an attitude and shoulders that swam with muscle as he strutted around town — quick and nasty in spurts that were all the more deadly because his normal pace was cool-dude slow motion. Slumming now, he sniffed around Caboodle's hind quarters, eyeing me all the while. "You seem to be marking up my turf again, Bay Street. Without a permit."

Caboodle kept her focus, and the entire top half of her body, on the innards of the garbage can. "Actually, I have tenant's rights, here," I sniffed, "by agreement with the landlord." I gestured with my head toward the Chicken Alley, confident of Jersey's ability to impress even the most arrogant tom. "You, sir, are a mere trespasser." It was true. His companion Has-being was a squeegee kid addicted to street drugs — a runaway from Montreal who slept over subway grates and under the Rosedale Bridge.

Baudelaire laughed and began hobbling toward us. I had calculated that I could count on him if things turned physical. But a single blind growl from Tantôt sent the old poet back to the wall.

"Listen, Mouthpiece." Tantôt had turned his full attention to Yours Subject to Leasehold. "This land belongs to me and mine."

"Ah, here we go," Baudelaire sneered from his corner. "Now he's gonna bore us with that old fairy tale how he's descended from the First Nations — from Louis Riel's favourite cat, no less." The venerable feline hacked away in a fit of pleurisy. I always figured the Riel malarkey was part of Tantôt's strategy for dethroning the older tom as lion king, particularly in these sexual wars. Tantôt knew that Baudelaire traced his family history back to his namesake poet, or at least to the tortoiseshell owned by the poet who wrote not just that famous *Drunken Boat* poem, but several surrealist verses devoted to *felis sylvestris*:

> I see my wife in spirit. Her regard,
> Like yours, amiable creature,
> Profound and cold, cuts and splits like snake tongues dart —

my translation, from what I have heard His Lordship quote of *Le Chat* while describing those daggers Penny Mariner has taken to casting at him with her own midlife regard.

Anyway, on his side Tantôt suddenly had found blood kinship with the notorious Louis Riel, hanged in 1885 by the European settlers in Canada for his rabblerousing on behalf of the Métis — those like himself who were of mixed First Nations and European background. Rebel with a cause.

As far as Tantôt was concerned, aged Baudelaire didn't merit a reply or so much as a dismissive sneer. But I could see the flint catch fire in his fool's-gold eyes — "your handsome eyes," the human Baudelaire muses in *Le Chat*, "melding metal and agate." Glancing first at Caboodle, who still had her snout buried in the tallow can, he hissed his scorn at Yours Pacifically instead. "That's right. I'm descended from the Father of the Red River Rebellion. And it was Has-beings like that pompous old judge you pal around with who murdered the both of them, to steal our land and everything on it."

"Give it a rest, will you, kid?" I spat. "What's the point of refighting lost tribal battles? Our kind was officially multicultural long before the rest of the country went that way. Your own beloved mixed heritage is a tribute to mongrelism, no? — how we're all the same and stronger for it."

"Bosh!" Baudelaire managed to splutter between tubercular spasms. Unfortunately, I had misjudged his native reluctance to mellow with age. *"Foutaise!"* he spat. Not exactly the support I was expecting. Withdrawing her head at last from the garbage can, her snout coated with kitchen grease and bread crumbs like one of Jersey's chicken wings, Caboodle favoured me with a question: "Purely moggy yourself, then, are ya, Alley cat? Gypsy disguised as boulevardier tenant? *Clochard?"*

"Vagabond," Baudelaire hisses. "Street urchin. With airs that he's superior to *nous autres*."

What am I to say? I was, in fact, born in an alley, behind a strip-mall delicatessen in Kensington Market. My mother was killed there, crushed by a delivery van when I was still a mewling kit. But I am no more immune to the green-eyed monster than all those Has-beings in Jersey's bar, not to mention the jealous Mrs. His Lordship Mariner. Instinctively, against my better judgment, I am drawn into the competition for Caboodle's favours, the biological imperative of self-assertion. Looking contemplatively into the cold, starless urban-winter sky, I assert: "Well, as you ask, I, too, am of distinguished heritage. It's said, in fact, that my litter descends directly from Dick Whittington's cat."

Of course this wasn't said at all. Called upon to improvise, I suddenly had thought of a lithograph His Lordship keeps in chambers, a drawing of the front of Newgate Prison. Today it is the site of London's Central Criminal Court, better known as the Old Bailey. But in 1437, Whittington's estate helped renovate the prison, Newgate, that stood there. In real life Whittington had been the Rockefeller of his day, a fantastically wealthy textiles merchant, wily lender to several monarchs, and London's mayor on three separate occasions. Government records record that Newgate had become "feble, over litle and so contagious of Eyre, yat hit caused the deth of many men." Legend turned Whittington into an orphan who made his fortune by selling his sole asset, his cat, as a mouser to a vermin-infested African potentate previously unfamiliar with *felis sylvestris*. And some say — without the slightest justification — that the feline carved on the front of the renovated Newgate, and featured prominently in the lithograph on Justice Mariner's wall, is Dick Whittington's legendary cat.

I call him Newgate — and now it is old Newgate I call upon

to rescue my reputation as a creature of low origins and limited appeal as a mate on the Yorkville bar scene. Unfortunately, my perjurious claim of a blood relationship with London's most famous lord mayor backfires. Suddenly, I am the common Anglicized enemy of two francophone alley cats, two dominant toms already half-mad with the scent of an ovulating queen in her prime. Like a Has-being cop in the middle of a ghetto "domestic," bingo, I'm the target of everyone's seething emotions.

They come at me from two sides as I run for the Alley's back doorway, whistling "God Save the Queen." Tantôt gets to me first, slapping at my left ear, which fortunately he merely clips and frays with a couple of claws. In trying to evade his razored roundhouse, I run full tilt into poor old Baudelaire coming ponderously at me from the other direction, all three of us yowling and spitting the while. Baudelaire sinks both his enfeebled forepaws into my neck, more to hang on for dear life than to inflict grievous bodily harm. Probably his real intent had been to break up the affray. Anyway, the force of our collision sends us rolling through the garbage and spilt vehicle fluids as we howl like banshees on fire. Arse over teakettle we fly through the dark, locked in each other's fetid embrace, and I feel I must die of suffocation. Baudelaire's mangy fur is ripe with kitchen waste and all the misery of his self-con-scious decay. At one and a half spins, the battered old moggy crashes head first into the wooden garbage bin belonging to the condominium building next to Jersey's club. I land on top of him, cushioned by the self-same bag of old bones, crushing the rancid air out of his lungs with a sad, doggish woof. His body skids into the bin, with his spine taking the brunt of it, and the noise of our doings is like to wake the dead. I scramble to my feet to find

Baudelaire lying motionless, a torn and rotting lettuce leaf draped like a winding-sheet over one still shoulder. Flexing my bleeding neck, and drawing back my lips in a vain if not ridiculous warning to Tantôt that worse lies in store for him, I catch sight of the instigator Caboodle fleeing the scene with a flirtatious smirk. *Taking lessons from Joyless Almundy, perhaps?* Eyeing first Baudelaire then my panting self, Tantôt backs toward the gate, and skitters into the night, just as Jersey blasts huge and raging through the Alley's back door, brandishing a potato in one hand as projectile, and a small head of radicchio in the other.

Only I am left standing, abject, over my old comrade of the streets. In a low mutter and winding up to throw his browning radicchio, Jersey asks me don't he already have enough damn fussing going on in his place here, murder investigations and the police in his business all day and night driving him over the speed limit to the poorhouse, now there's mayhem and mutilation out the back and at four o'clock ay em in the morning, besides. "Good for nothin' black cat," he spits. "Brung me nothin' but bad luck ever since you and Your Honour's Sorry-Ass Refugee Road Show sashayed into my place here, without no reservations, neither." Eyes wide with unfocussed panic (and plenty of reservations), I glance apologetically at my landlord and mew a shame-faced adieu — to both him and my old mucker Baudelaire, by way of the latter's namesake:

Thy fecund loins sparkle most magical
While gold-dusted sand
Starlights vaguely thy gaze so mystical.

(Translation copyright Amicus, Q.C., for Quixotic Combatant; all rights reserved.) Then I low-tail it east up Cumberland, watching my bleeding back, an outlaw. At Bay Street I break into a loping feline gallop, running for downtown — running, once more, for my life.

Dead at the Chicken Alley

(Andante)

CHAPTER 6

He's Funny That Way

His name was Gaunt and he looked it — pallid, skinny, google-eyed behind his beer-bottle spectacles, indulging much too often in the nervous habit of dislocating his double-jointed jaws, a Moose Jaw, Saskatchewan, boy lost in the big city. To look at him you wouldn't imagine that on his bedroom wall hung a framed scrap of vellum alleging he was "duly Called to the Degree of Barrister-at-Law and was admitted to practice at the Bar of Her Majesty's Courts in Ontario."

Readers of my previous adventures will recognize Leland Gaunt as he strolls bow-legged as a roughrider into the Alley, at lunchtime on the Saturday after Des Cheshire's arrest. Gaunt had preceded Nadia Hussein as Justice Mariner's clerk at the Court of Appeal (or the judge's co-clerk, counting me, of course), and he served as winning counsel in the Slovenskaya murder case. Though successful on that occasion, the possibility that it might have ended otherwise, with Her Majesty providing Katrina bed and breakfast for the next twenty-five years, had scared him out of criminal litigation. These days, Gaunt was studying for his master's degree at Osgoode Hall Law School, in the suburban wilds of North York. To pay the bills, he taught a research course to first-year students at the law school, and he took on freelance devilling — research and other dogsbody work for senior lawyers. It was in the latter capacity that Justice Mariner had invited him down to the Alley for lunch.

Having escaped lawful custody, I was not present for this particular colloquy, so I have had to reconstruct it from what I heard later. Over Jersey's Alley Chicken Satay with Chicky-Sticky Rice (vegetarian-style for Leland Gaunt), the judge naturally would have inquired, "On your way in, you didn't happen to notice that bloody cat I've inherited, did you? The one they kept in the library at Osgoode Hall?"

"You 'inherited' it?" Gaunt asks, dislocating his jaw and putting on the goofy face that makes him look philosophical, he thinks.

"For my sins," His Lordship says. But of course he misses me. "The pesky bugger's absconded. Haven't seen him since yesterday afternoon. Jersey caught him fighting in the alley and he ran off. I've spent half the morning looking for the little pest."

Gaunt gets a pained look that is meant to pass for bemusement. "Amicus. Little Amicus Curious, I used to call him."

Reason number one we never really got on.

"*Adversarius*, more like. Enemy of the court." Old joke. Justice Mariner doesn't mean it. He's worried about me. He shakes his head and suddenly looks like he's really about to weep. "Jersey says good riddance. But it seems like everybody's leaving me, lately, Lee, as though the cliché's true: Old lawyers never die, they just lose their appeal. Nobody loves me."

After a long, uncomfortable pause, Gaunt says tentatively, "I'm here, Judge."

The judge stares at the table, then shrugs and smiles gamely. "He'll come back when he comes back, I guess." Okay, maybe he's not *that* worried about me. "Anyhow, on to the *ratio decidendi* — the heart of the case, why I've asked you down here today, Lee. And thanks for coming, by the way. You know the musician Des Cheshire?"

"Know him? I've got every one of his recordings. The ones with Billy Wonder, and his other ones, too. With Jim Hall, Lionel Hampton. All of them. I play a little jazz trumpet, myself, you know. Or used to. In junior high school band."

"I know you're a man of hidden talents." Buried, I'd say. "Well, the thing is, Lee, believe it or not, Des has been charged with killing Wonder."

"You're kidding."

The judge stares at his former clerk, who finally says, "No, I guess you wouldn't be, would you? Not about that. But why would Des Cheshire kill the goose that laid the golden egg?"

The judge shrugs. "Maybe for that exact reason. Apparently Billy very much had the upper hand in their business dealings. Des's been in his shadow since day one."

Gaunt considers this, then nods. "And Wonder gets all of the public credit, except among the *cognoscenti.*"

"You mean all those lonely subscribers to *Downbeat* jazz magazine, like your good self, I suppose."

Gaunt chooses to ignore the sarcasm. "So it was professional jealousy?"

"That's the theory, I guess, although it probably wasn't entirely professional. It was very personal, I'm sure." His Lordship gets that ominous far-away look that signifies he is about to quote the Classics. "'O! beware my lord, of jealousy; / It is the green-ey'd monster which doth mock / The meat it feeds on.'"

"Romeo and Juliet?" It is an old game poor Gaunt feels compelled to play with the judge, who loves bullying all comers over his familiarity with Great Litrichoor, and particularly the Bard. Name That Tragedy.

"Dead wrong as usual, Lee. Too much time in the law library, not enough outings to the Stratford Festival. I'm surprised you don't know that one, though. It's from *Othello*."

"Still. Murder! Des Cheshire, the Great White Hope of the alto saxophone."

"Yes, well, that really brings us to my point here, Lee. I've met Des, and, to be honest, well, let's just say the Crown could make a pretty good case against him. On the other hand, let's also say I have a reasonable doubt about his involvement. Of course, I personally cannot take or make the case . . ."

"Oh, now, Judge, you know I've retired from the battlefield."

"Retired? After your famous victory in your very first defence file? Retired? Surely, sir, you jest. An advocate of your skills, retired before he's begun? You've just gone back to the reserves, waiting for the call to active duty in a deserving cause." His Lordship cambers his eyebrows. "And Cheshire has the brass to make it worth your while, Lee."

"Really, Judge, I could use the money, sure enough, but . . ."

"Not to mention the PR. *And* the experience. Lee, a case like this comes along once, at most twice, in a criminal defence counsel's career."

"But that's just it, Judge. I'm not a criminal defence counsel. I just don't have enough experience to take it on." *Or the stomach.* "Even if I were in practice, it's out of my league. I'm not like you."

"How can you say that, Lee? A few months ago, you won a first-degree murder prosecution that looked hopeless. With a very experienced Crown lawyer on the other side. And I'll be right behind you again, just like that time. We'll work on everything together, behind the scenes of course. It'll be a blast, eh? You'll be the advocate, I'll be your junior — in a case that will do absolute wonders, so to say, for your legal career."

"Or absolutely sink it, once and for all."

Of course, at the best of times it is hard for a lawyer to say no to a judge of the highest court in the province. And then the judge humbles himself, besides, offering to "junior" for his own former student. Poor Gaunt is flattered, badgered, and persuaded all at once. His ego is too fragile for the assault, his instinct for survival not finely enough tuned. Ignorant to the last of Shakespeare, he is oblivious that discretion is the better part of valour. "It's going to be in all the papers, judge. I'm going to need all the help from you I can get. I'm going to hold you to it. You can't leave me alone out there."

"Of course not," His Lordship says, signalling with a pout that the very idea is absurd. "Even though an advocate of your abilities will need no guidance of any significance, I'm sure." He turns toward the bar. "The other half of my friend's Shirley Temple, barkeep."

Jersey responds with his laser glare, then cocks his head with the same air of menace, even after Justice Mariner adds, "Pretty please?"

Trying to calm himself, Gaunt smiles woodenly and surveys the nearly empty club. "You used to work here, eh?"

"Long, long ago, Lee. In 'my salad days, when I was green in judgment.'"

The smile flickers from Gaunt's face, the poor sod. He sips at his ginger ale with grenadine and he grimaces. "*Othello*, right?"

"Actually, the other play about sexual jealousy: *Antony and Cleopatra*."

"Like I said, Judge. I'm going to need you right behind me, all the way."

"I know, Lee. I know."

CHAPTER 7

Seems Like Old Times

Goodwill. We all rely on it, and sometimes we profit by it in very concrete ways: a good Samaritan offers us a bed for the night, and maybe her leftover tuna salad, a ride downtown . . . any of which would have come in handy for Yours Footloose after I departed the Alley on that fateful eve. But to Has-being number crunchers, goodwill is an "intangible asset," the good reputation and customer loyalty attached to a business.

It's a matter of capital, in other words, and, inevitably there are lawsuits over its monetary valuation. During my residency at the Great Library of Osgoode Hall, I regularly dozed on law reports concerning business goodwill, in tomes left lying open in the sun as it filtered through the cathedral-style windows of the Reading Room. Take, for example, page twenty-five in volume two of the British *King's Bench Reports* for 1934, if memory serves. His Majesty's judges recount there how the Whiteman Smith Motor Company had reached the end of its lease on the garage it operated. The garage owners were worried that in moving they would lose the goodwill attached to the premises. So they sued their landlord for the prospective loss. Lord Scrutton ruled there were three kinds of goodwill: dog goodwill, rat goodwill, and cat goodwill. With dog goodwill, Lord Scrutton said, the customers followed the person to the new place of business (tails wagging indiscriminately, no doubt). The rats were those who drifted sniffily from home to home (or garage to garage), all greed, without distinct loyalty. And the cats preferred the old home to the person who kept it. They stayed with the business even when it changed hands.

Bull! you will reply, adding one more animal to the menagerie, if you are a companion human of sensitivity. If you love the resident cat, the resident cat loves you back, albeit no more uncritically than members of your own species or family. As Lord Maugham notes in his separate opinion in *Whiteman Smith, felis sylvestris* may be attracted away from his old home by someone who is kind and caring — "by a gentle stroke on the back and the promise of a bowl of milk." That, after all, is how I ended up at the Chicken Alley, never mind that its milk has now soured. The dog is lauded for its loyalty and "unconditional love," but again, as *felis sylvestris* knows from centuries of bitter experience, well, you heard it here second: discretion is the better part of valour.

Still, I cannot in conscience affirm that Lord Scrutton is totally wrong. For I must admit that Time and Fortune have fetched me up at my old digs again, preferring the house to the householder. Heartily out of puff, desperately tired, my dogs howling at the early morning sun after my long trot from the Alley, I find myself at the northeast entrance of Osgoode Hall, in that little-used alleyway between the building's northerly wall and the court-house, one of those eerily quiet no-man's-lands common even in the busiest downtown neighbourhoods: the haunts of waifs, strays, and muggers.

Waif and stray, I loiter in the frigid midwinter air for someone, *anyone*, Fate preserve us, to open the door so that I can sneak past security and scoot upstairs to the Great Library, my home before the Alley. And there I plan to lie low once more until this Baudelaire business blows over. For I am certain that among my Great Librarians I will find subsisting goodwill toward the former cat in residence. Unfortunately, at the moment the matter of my homecoming remains, as lawyers like to say, moot. In lieu of clucking and cooing librarians, I am met by the muggers — a vigilante posse of my own temperamental kind.

That's the one. A lanky tom shows his canines as the group slinks its way up the sidewalk. The leader, of course, is the vain and testosterone-crazed Tantôt, the dominant male whose younger limbs have brought him here before me. *Sucker-punched old Baudelaire*, he calls over his shoulder, to two of his thug buddies. *Blatant regicide, it was. Whacked a weak old moggy who posed no threat to his gene pool at all.*

You'd have thought I'd done Tantôt a favour, declawing — and dethroning — Baudelaire once and for all. But of course nature obliges him to challenge me as the official slayer of the old king and thereby as official pretender to Baudelaire's alpha-male throne. So here *(sigh)* we go again. A lynch mob. The stereotypical, highly uncivilized (not to say banal) cat fight. More highly evolved and learned in the art of advocacy, I make my opening address to the kangaroo court: *Lads, lads. Whatever happened to the old presumption of innocence? The cause before us was simply a tragic accident. We were long-time friends, the deceased and I, a fact widely known to those, well, those in the know. We were at a nightclub, and, as occasionally happens in such premises, an affray broke out. High spirits amid spirits inducing highs and all that. Personally, I struck no blow, uttered no threat, bespoke no menace. I promise you. A jealous, pheromone-drunk young tom* (I studiously ignore their leader) *came at me daggers drawn, drunk on his own hormones. I merely stepped out of harm's way, friends, as you gentlemen would have done your-selves, I am sure, in the circumstances. Danger to life and limb and so on. Live and let live, after all, is the motto of the scholar as well as the gentleman. So I merely turned the other jowl, as I say, and in so doing, well, it was pure misadventure, what we gentlemen barristers call unavoidable accident. Totally non-compensable in negligence, not to say unreachable by Her Majesty's criminal courts. Unavoidably, and sadly, in just turning aside I collided with the venerable Master Baudelaire, esteemed by us all — or, really, to be precise, he collided with me, as in the chaos of the mêlée and with old Baudelaire in his dotage, he bumbled all befogged and befuddled in my direction. So you see, if there was fault, it was totally attributable to the poor departed old loved one. Contributory negligence, we call it, in the pro-fession. We collided, Baudelaire and Yours Regretfully. We fell to the earth. The late, lamented poet struck his skull on a garbage bin. And that was all he wrote, so to speak. Happenstance. Total misfortune. Pure unavoidable accident.* Unconvinced that I have reached the hearts and minds of the jury, I conclude: *Fellas. Guys. I was lucky to escape with my own neck, I assure you.*

You got that right, Tantôt hisses.

I have not, in fact, swayed the triers of fact, who also appear to be judge and hangman as they slink toward me all sinew and synapse, as of one body but from three sides, the feline equivalent of the three-headed hound at Hell's gate. Trapped at the wall, I push my snout against the big, black Law Society door, but it offers no quarter. I turn to fight for my life, adrenaline reducing my vision to the pure electric movement around me. The blood thrums in my ears, half-deafening me to the chorus of cater-wauling (including my own) that raises the stench of blood in our nostrils, though none is yet spilt.

My assailants spring at me, and at the same moment the door opens. Tantôt caroms off its front edge as his foot soldiers scatter into the yard and I hightail it into the corridor, ducking effort-lessly as another old nemesis, Roman Nobb, Q.C., a Law Society bencher who shows me no persisting goodwill at all, kicks at me fecklessly, cursing me under his breath, as he tries to step outside over my hurtling form.

✣

Actually, of course, I don't hightail it at all. Hugging the wain-scoting and quarter-round floor trim, I skitter past the security guards, very much at low tail. (Have you ever, after all, seen a spooked cat — or dog, come to that — flee for its life with its tail in the come-and-get-me position?) Then I gallop at full tilt through one of those metal scanners that look like a pretend doorway in a minimalist production by an impecunious theatre company.

Slowing only a little, it's up the stairs and into the library, where I am briefly cooed upon, sure enough, by my old friends Katrina Slovenskaya and Elise Throckmorton, assistant and research librarian respectively. And it doesn't hurt a bit. However, my refugee application is soon denied, their boss and head librarian Elizabeth Bane sniffling into the Reference Room with a tissue pressed to her red nose. "Aha. I thought my allergies were kicking up!" says she, and summarily orders me re-deported. Even here I am become *feles non grata*, futilely pleading, *How can you accuse my kind of inconstancy when in fact it is human cruelty and rejection which makes gypsies of us?* Deaf as Tantôt to my philosophy, dear Katrina Slovenskaya gathers me up, clasping me to what her romance novels would describe as an ample bosom and sighing over me the while. *Yes, I've missed you, too,* I purr, not without sincerity, and the poor old darling begins to shed big, fat tears of mingled joy and despair. She transports me to the stairs, where suddenly I wriggle free (crying, *No offence, dear Kate!*), push off one of those ample thingamies of hers, pull a one-eighty, land on all fours, and scrabble for Justice Mariner's chambers on the fourth floor.

Along the way, I ponder again how the legal concept of cat goodwill is rife with ambiguity. You can definitely smell trouble in the wind, after all, when people and their pets all crowd into the business law reports and are not always housebroken, with their cat goodwill and dog goodwill and rat goodwill, and then Lord Justice Maugham comes along and introduces a rabbit, if I remember correctly ("the customers who come simply from propinquity"; see page fifty of said *King's Bench Reports* and please don't ask Yours Jurisprudently to distinguish the rabbits from the rats). Indeed, as my former accidental library researches revealed, after a dozen or so years of animal metaphors in goodwill cases, the English Court of Appeal began wrinkling its nose. Called upon to value a leasehold for an antiques shop, Lord Evershed remarks that "the phrase 'cat' goodwill . . . is apt to be misleading. . . . If it is true that a cat has nine lives, we express the hope that in relation to the *Landlord and Tenant Act* it has lived the last of them and may now be decently interred."[*]

Amen, and *requiescat in pace*. When I reach the fourth floor, happily the door to His Lordship's chambers is ajar. I stand stock-still just to right of the door frame, discerning that the way is safe. A large book and many papers are spread out on the judge's desk, but the ancient Mariner himself is absent. Perhaps he is off consulting his clerk Nadia, or Seeing a Man About a Dog or something. I dart inside, and the clatter of approaching Has-being footsteps immediately sends me scampering behind some volumes on the judge's bookshelf. Peeking around a colourfully bound treatise entitled *Where There's Life, There's Lawsuits*, I observe Nadia Hussein enter with a mug of herbal tea. She makes herself at home on His Lordship's beloved chair — the armchair previously owned by John Beverley Robinson and gifted by Penny and Mariner *filles* to old Ted on his appointment to the Court of Appeal, the same chair somewhat crudely reupholstered when I imagined that by removing the leather cover I could render it less cruel and unusual on the flank of *felis sylvestris* and *Homo allegedly sapiens*, both. Unfortunately, the Court did not agree.

Sitting tall now on the restored antique, articling student Hussein is indeed a very handsome, even regal female of medium height, jet black hair, and clear, smooth complexion. Looking at her nicely-proportioned, intelligent face and her trim form, you can understand Penny Mariner's jealousy. At the moment, Hussein wears spectacles pushed down to the tip of her dainty

---

[*]*Mullins v. Wessex Motors Ltd.*, [1947] 2 *All England Reports*, page 729.

brown nose. As she makes a note from the book, the parchment-pallid Leland Gaunt darkens the lintel.

Yet he does not enter. He waits until Hussein looks up, then asks her, "And you would be?"

"Mr. Justice Mariner's articled clerk." She says it "clark," *à la mode anglaise*, widening her black eyes at her visitor. "And you would be?"

"Mr. Justice Mariner's articled clerk as was." Gaunt says it "clerk," *à la mode canadienne*, then dislocates and relocates his jaw, quick and easy as you like. "Last year."

"Oh, yes. Mr. Gaunt." Hussein nods curtly at Gaunt, then returns to her notes.

"I'm afraid the judge has given me the use of this office, his office."

"Don't be afraid, Mr. Gaunt." Hussein does not look up from her work. "It is very cosy, indeed."

"No. What I mean, Ms. . . . ?"

The articled clerk finally takes in her predecessor, who has not moved from the doorway. "Hussein. Nadia Hussein."

"What I mean, Nadia, is that I need to use it now."

"So do I, Mr. Gaunt. You see, I am working on a very urgent file. It's a matter of first-degree murder. The famous musician, Mr. Desmond Cheshire. He is a friend of Mr. Justice Mariner, it would seem."

Gaunt actually puts his hands on his hips, and after doing the business with his jaw again, with a rather alarming click at the joint, he whines in exasperation, "But that's *my* file! That's what I've come all the way down here in killer traffic to work on. It's *my* file."

"And mine, sir. I am deputized to assist you."

"Who says?"

"His Honour says."[*] Hussein lifts one side of the book slightly off the desktop. "I've borrowed a pathology treatise from the library, you see. I am reading all about garrotting, Mr. Gaunt."

Out of politeness, for he is a vegetarian from Moose Jaw, Gaunt raises an eyebrow.

"It is very interesting, indeed. It seems that these days females are more often the victims of ligature strangulation, as the literature calls it. But at one time the state authorities used it in Spain and Portugal to execute convicted felons. The term *garrotte* comes from the Spanish for 'cudgel,' you see, signifying the stick that these fellows, these executioners or whatever, they would twist it behind your neck to tighten the wire or cord, to strangle you, should you be so unlucky, Mr. Gaunt. Later, they designed a sort of metal collar, it says here, with a screw in it." Hussein looks up brightly at Gaunt and smiles as she makes a noise with her tongue as of a human neck breaking. "You know, that's really getting screwed, isn't it, Mr. Gaunt?"

Gaunt turns mushy-pea green. "Well, okay then, I suppose. Yes. Okay. I guess I can just use the library then, myself. For now.

[*]Student Hussein falls in with the modern practice, recently mandated by our Chief Justice, of evicting lords and ladies from our courtrooms. This is supposed to be very democratic, using His or Her Honour for all justices, instead of Lordship and Ladyship. In my view — which perhaps you will find snooty as befits a cat and mere quadruped — it detracts from the necessary dignity of our law and its historic roots in the British and French legal systems. I believe tradition, and history, inculcate respect — such as Gaunt and Hussein seem to lack one for the other.

Yes. That should work — for today or whatnot. And I was just about to suggest that you look into the garrotting. I mean, we've got the preliminary hearing coming up, don't we? Pathology. Garrotting. Yes. Get started on that, will you? Good."

Bowed silently again over her work, Nadia Hussein studies the physiological hows and whys of garrotting. Leland Gaunt never gets past the threshold of Justice Mariner's office. Immediately that he leaves, the articling student claps her beautiful brown hands and barks with laughter.

CHAPTER 8

Can I Get a Witness?

FORM 17

Warrant for witness

Canada,
Province of Ontario,
Judicial District of York.

To the peace officers of Canada, its provinces, and territories:

Whereas *Eugene Desmond Cheshire of New York, New York, USA*, has been charged that he did, on or about the *thirteenth* day of *January, 2005*, at *the City of Toronto* in the said *Judicial District of York, cause the death of William Merridew Wonder and thereby commit murder in the first degree contrary to section 235(1) of the* Criminal Code;

And Whereas it has been made to appear that *Thomas a/k/a "Tommy" a/k/a "Doubting Tommy" Profitt*, of *no known address*, hereinafter called the witness, is likely to give material evidence for the prosecution and that

(a) the said Thomas Profitt will not attend unless compelled to do so;

(b) the said Thomas Profitt is evading service of a subpoena.

This is therefore to command you, in Her Majesty's name, to arrest and bring the witness forthwith before the Superior Court of Justice for Ontario to be dealt with in accordance with section 706 of the *Criminal Code*.

Dated this *21st* **day of** *March, 2005* **A.D., at** *Toronto, Ontario.*

(signed) *Conchita M. Presenkowski,*
A clerk of the Court

CHAPTER 9

The Trill Is Gone

There is something feline about Melody Pepino. Half Filipina, half Italian, the twenty-eight-year-old assistant Crown is all of five-foot nothing and maybe ninety-five pounds sopping wet. Despite her petite stature and relative youth, or maybe because of them, there is an electricity about her, a lithe, olive-skinned voltage that commands respect. Her faded skirts (she subsists on a government salary, after all) sing against her sharp-winged pelvis and tight little derriere as her heels clack spitefully — one-two, one-two — through courthouse hallways, giving her the air of a not quite used-up slattern. And this personal fashion statement — *Don't even think about it!* — is confirmed by the look of angry suspicion on her bony, heavily made-up face. Within minutes of meeting her, it is clear she conducts office hours on the theory that as a small, young, female double-ethnic, she must Fight Or Die.

To be fair, most Crown counsel get something of that hunted look about them. Hungry and hunted all at once. It's an occupational hazard. *Who's predator, who's prey?* But when Pepino suggests to Gaunt that we waive our right to a preliminary inquiry — a first-stage hearing to determine whether the Crown has enough evidence to go to a full jury trial against Des Cheshire — Gaunt doesn't dare reject the idea outright.

In fact, we on the defence side are keen for the hearing: We want to test the Crown's case and particularly the quality of its witnesses. Besides, we're slated for the docket of Mr. Justice Hernando Cactus, whom Justice Mariner assures us is not at all prickly. "He's actually a very sweet, reasonable fellow," His Lordship has said. "Refreshing — more like the juice than the thorns. Urbane, literate. He might even have heard of Des, and he'll appreciate his intelligence and humour."

Gaunt nodded, cocking his jaw. "I hear he's fair. Balanced."

"A dog man, apparently," the judge replied, as though this were necessarily a positive attribute. Of course Justice Mariner is something of a caninophile himself, never mind that Stong, his idiot golden retriever, is now in Penny Mariner's sole custody and I am actually the loyal companion animal — never mind again that, at the moment, I had secreted myself behind the divan in his chambers. At the time I was not sure which His Lordship missed more — mutt or missus. "His wife died last year," he told Gaunt wistfully of Justice Cactus, "so it's just him, poor old sod, and his beloved pooch. A beagle called Legal, apparently."

What is this with dogs and joke-names? Still, I don't suppose courthouse cats called Amicus for *amicus curiae* should throw stones.

"You drag us through a prelim., it'll just mean that much more delay," Pepino now warns Leland Gaunt, with a look of mild disgust, "while your celebrity client cools his heels in the nasty old Don Jail." Her dark eyes seem never to rest, always on the lookout while never ceasing to take your measure. "I mean, if you really think you'll get him off on this." She snorts, and looks off into space, all thrumming and electric.

"I don't know, Melody," Gaunt answers. Pepino stands intimidatingly close to him in his "personal space," resting a stack of files on the table in the Great Library Reading Room. I have sneaked back there to sleep in the sun beside Gaunt's briefcase, at his feet, still lying low, as it were, having just cadged lunch off Modesto, the sous-chef in the Barrister's Dining Room hard by. Apparently under the impression that I am back in lawful residence at the library, Gaunt has scratched my ears with the greeting, "Lost and found, eh, Amicus Curious? The rover returns." "I wouldn't want to deprive you of the chance to test your case," he now tells Pepino. "I mean, heck, I'd think even now, in the early going, you'd want to drop it down to manslaughter. At the very least. Before it gets really embarrassing. We're talking about an important artist here, a peaceable intellectual."

Gaunt probably thinks this is a smooth move, but in fact Pepino smells blood. I can see her nostrils flare. "You offering to plead your guy out?" She barks with fake laughter.

"Shhh!" an angry-looking woman in barrister's robes shushes from the next table.

Realizing he has shown his flank, Gaunt shakes his head so hard that I hear something rattle. "No way. No way. We're sticking with not guilty. In fact, I honestly expect you'll decide to withdraw the charges altogether before we even set a trial date." Gaunt folds his arms to prove it, but Melody Pepino doesn't so much as glance at him.

"Oh, yeah. That'll happen." There's not even the play of smile on her lips as she snorts again and her eyes dart about, as though the entire Toronto criminal defence bar were waiting to pounce from behind the Doric columns and oak bookcases and reference inquiry desks.

"In the long run, it'd save the A-G resources, not to mention the taxpayer. I mean, I'm sure you've got plenty of real criminals to prosecute, Mel."

Finally, Pepino gives Gaunt her full, wide-eyed attention, for effect's sake, of course. "Oh, yeah? You representing the auditor-general, too? Celebrity nightclub murderers aren't enough for you and your vast experience at the criminal bar?"

Low blow, and Gaunt clearly feels it. "No, I'm serious, Melody. I think this is a waste of Her Majesty's very valuable time."

Pepino tilts her head and rolls her eyes, showing to their worst effect the big black lines she has drawn around them. *The Dragon Lady.* "Oh, I'm sure she can fit you and your horn-tooter into her diary, between knighting some cokehead rock star" — she flexes her drawn-on eyebrows at the quailing Leland Gaunt — "and putting dents in the taxpayers' newest battleship with her champagne bottle."

Gaunt stands and begins backing away, stumbling against his chair before putting some distance between himself and the irritable assistant Crown.

"Hey, shush!" the lady barrister shushes again, causing everyone else in the vast, echoing room to look up from their highly expensive work.

"Anyways, Melody," Gaunt whispers, "if you don't mind, I think we'll go with the prelim. I mean, first-degree murder. How you're going to prove that . . ."

"Mind? Why should I mind, Leland? You wanna show me

your hand, that's up to you." Pepino, who has not bothered to lower her voice, scowls at the shusher. She shifts her load of files, preparing to leave, knowing full well that we don't have to show her anything. Rather, she is obliged to disclose all her evidence so we can make full answer and defence, as the case law puts it. She shrugs, staring at Gaunt with a look of sullen boredom. "It's your funeral."

⁓੭੭⁓

Justice Mariner felt really guilty about meeting Donna Nippelman at Pasta La Vista (Fusion Cuisine with a Latin Accent). It was the new place he and Mrs. Mariner had been planning to try for dinner just before Penny evicted him. But the thing with Nippelman was just a friendly lunch, in broad daylight, and Pasta La Vista was the only place that came into the judge's head when, his heart racing, his voice a full tone higher than normal, he breathlessly connected with his old girlfriend over the phone from chambers.

That is where I learn about the luncheon, after it is all over but the crying. I lay in my quarters behind the divan, sifting and organizing the various data from the fallout as His Lordship deals with it in further, yet more strained, phone conversations — conversations with his wife and, subsequently, Isadore "Izzy" Finster, the noted divorce lawyer.

"But, Pen, I'm telling you, I was, you know, just checking the place out, for us, you and me, because we were thinking of trying it. And the whole truth and nothing but the truth, I swear and affirm and attest it, Pen, honest to God, the fact is, I felt nothing for her. Absolutely *nada*. It was like an out-of-body experience and

I was watching myself do lunch with her. We had almost nothing to say to each other. I felt a little repulsed, even." The judge listens briefly, then cries, "Divorce? Penny, this is getting just a little out of hand, isn't it? I've told you, it was just lunch. And a lousy one, at that — as you well know. The first time we've seen each other in thirty years, at least, Donna and I. You want to throw away our whole life together over that? A one-off, over-priced nosh, in public, not all that different from a high school reunion?"

Mrs. Her Lordship is having none of it, but I could have assured her that what Justice Mariner says is absolutely true, judging from what he tells Izzy Finster after another couple of panicked hours waiting for the family law specialist to return his calls. "Things ain't what they used to be, Izzy. When we were dating all those years ago, Donna was an art history major. She was totally into it. In fact, she broke up with me when she decided to spend a year in Europe, Italy in particular, doing the museums and the galleries. She'd even spent six months taking Italian immersion classes — language courses. She didn't want any constraints, she said, nothing to compromise her freedom. So she dumped me. Now, Izzy, get this, now, she's married to some premiums-and-incentives magnate. No, no kidding, he sells pens and binders and plastic rulers, you know, yo-yos and memo pads, the sort of stuff they hand out at conventions and seminars with Your Corporate Name Here printed on them. Corporate *tchatchkies*. And they live way the heck out in Pickering or something. The quintessential suburbs. They've got two kids, mostly grown, of course, a pool, a koi pond, a cottage, two SUVs, his and hers, I guess. And she's not Nippelman any more, she's Porchnik. His Name There, so to speak, on old Donna Porchnik, formerly *artiste*, currently four-wheel-drive wife to southern Ontario's premiums and incentives magnate."

His Lordship laughs, somewhat desperately, it seems. "And I'm telling you, Iz, to quote that old Des Cheshire tune, the trill was gone. It was like we were from different planets. After the first five minutes, after we gave each other the *Readers' Digest* version of what we'd been doing for thirty years, we had nothing else to say. Zilcho. We were in two different universes."

Finster commiserates, empathizes and such, apparently.

"Well, that's just it. I mean, she's attractive enough for her age — *our* age, I guess. Still has her deviated septum, too." The judge laughs more sincerely. "And her spectacles still slip down her nose with perspiration. Who was it, Cézanne?, Gaugin?, who said he liked a woman who could sweat? I did, too, and we had that artsy joke about it. I mean, she was slender, but filled out, you know? She could sweat and a few other things, too. And that's still there — I could see what I saw in her. Voluptuous. Passionate. Hubba-hubba . . . not. Honestly, it's faded, you know, Iz, she's letting it go — she's domesticated. The trill is gone. She was flattered that I'd called, I could see that. But there was nothing there any more, and we both knew it." His Lordship sighs and looks at the ceiling. "I mean, holy moly, Iz, between you and me, there was no stirring in the nether regions. More like shrivelling, to make full disclosure of admitted facts. We both felt, well, deflated."

This is clearly more than Finster needs to know about Donna Porchnik, Donna Nippelman as was. He apparently tells Justice Mariner to admit nothing, then asks if the judge wants him to draft a separation agreement as a pre-emptive strike against Penny. "God no, not a separation agreement," Justice Mariner replies. "Jesus."

It might just scare her straight, Finster seems to suggest. Bring home the reality of it all and make her see sense. Get her to reconcile, before she cleans the judge out.

"And it might just be what she really wants," His Lordship grimly replies. "Then there's no turning back. *Fait accompli* and all that. The thing of it is, she saw me in Pasta La Vista with Donna, Iz, and she jumped to all the wrong conclusions."

Well, that wouldn't exactly be good news for us if push came to shove, Finster evidently observes.

"I wouldn't say that, exactly," the judge responds. "See, *she* was there with Hernando Cactus. . . . Yes, really, Mr. Justice Cactus, the Ontario Court's most eligible widower. And I'd had a few glasses of wine, see, to get myself through the Nippelman reunion. So I'm afraid I toddled right over to their table and I asked them exactly what they thought they were doing making a public display of wrecking my marriage. The green-eyed monster and all that, I suppose, helped along with a little *vin* more than ordinarily expensive. So of course Penny asked me what exactly I thought I was doing there with yet another of my 'frumpy floozies,' meaning poor, blameless Donna, of course.

"To be honest, before I went storming over there, I don't think they'd even seen us, so I guess I set the cat among the pigeons. They'd been too busy gazing into each other's limpid eyes to notice us, I suppose." His Lordship pauses and swallows. "What the hell's she playing at, Iz? I mean, she kicks me out, accepts luncheon dates with old geldings set out to pasture in the lower courts, then accuses me of infidelity. . . . Talk about the pot calling the kettle. . . . You know what? You're right. Let's go for it. Draft me that separation agreement. Let's serve it on her forthwith, as fast as you can get it drawn up. . . .

"The restaurant? Oh, yeah, sorry — yeah, there's definitely more to that. Unfortunately. Don't laugh. As I say, I'd had a little vino, things got a little heated with Cactus, who's more prickly than I thought, Iz. The upshot was, well, they threw me out of the place. No, I'm not shitting you. I wish I was. Hey, it's not that funny, man. . . .

"Yes, well, unfortunately Penny's divorce threat could be the least of my problems. . . . That's right. You might be getting a call about me from the Canadian Judicial Council. Matter of a little public affray at Pasta La Vista . . . I'm not sure I can altogether credit your optimism on that, Izzy. Anyway, poor Donna. She got stuck with the bill, including drinks and wine, man, and I never even had the chance to say goodbye, it's been a slice. Had to leave her at the table there, open-mouthed and staring over her warm white chocolate strudel with raspberry-mandarin coulis. What a mess. Nostalgia ain't what it used to be, is it, Izzy? The cost of living has just shot through the damn roof."

CHAPTER 10

This Could Be the Start of Something Big

Each side in a trial has its theory of the case, the essence of what it must prove to come out the winner. Melody Pepino has inscribed her theory in mascara, in capital letters, on the inside cover of the notebook she has prepared for *The Queen against Eugene Desmond Cheshire*. Having made my way over to the courthouse at 362 University via the underground tunnel from Osgoode Hall, I have taken up my accustomed place under the stenographer's table at the foot of the bench (if I keep still, generally I am indulged), and I can see Pepino's little outline clearly:

<u>AGEING LIONS</u>
— SEX.
— JEALOUSY.
— GREED.
(Men will be boys)

To the jury, Pepino elaborates that she and her learned colleague, Gordon Mortimer, will demonstrate that Des Cheshire and the deceased, Billy Wonder, had been feuding for decades.

They started out in the music business as friends, penniless and idealistic, but, as with a bad marriage, familiarity bred contempt. And success made them enemies. She will prove that "an airtight contract drafted by Billy's lawyers and agents prevented the accused man, Des Cheshire, from working with any other leader — the agreement bound him, members of the jury, to what lawyers call a non-compete clause. Des Cheshire, you will learn, tends to call it the white slave-trade clause."

Pepino fixes the jury with a grim regard as they stare back in fascinated horror at her waist, where she clasps one hand in the other so hard that the claspee goes bloodless. "You know, an English judge once wrote, 'This contract is so one-sided, I'm surprised to find it written on both sides of the page.' That was how Mr. Cheshire felt about his contract with Billy Wonder, ladies and gentlemen. This contract that Mr. Cheshire so despised, this indentured slave document entitled Mr. Wonder to seventy-five percent of any royalties regarding music Mr. Cheshire wrote for Mr. Wonder and his groups. As the band became popular, and even found itself on the hit parade, the royalties became a significant amount of money, money out of Mr. Cheshire's pocket, straight into Mr. Wonder's. And on top of that, most of the general public thought Mr. Wonder was the author of those popular, money-making tunes. Mr. Wonder got all the credit for Mr. Cheshire's chart-topping music."

The judge, Mr. Justice Oliver Honey of the Ontario Superior Court of Justice, glances over at Des Cheshire in the prisoner's dock, I suppose to see what effect Pepino's address works on him. Where Justice Cactus is mostly not prickly, Justice Honey's approach is all vinegar. As Des Cheshire will say of Oliver Honey at the morning break, with mock charity, perhaps: "Well, who wants to attract more flies, anyway?" Fat, dyspeptic, bald as a turtle's egg, and well beyond his best-before date as a disinterested arbiter of Her Majesty's causes, Justice Honey scowls down from the bench like a truffle-snuffling ungulate. For his part, clad in a checked sport coat and his inevitable orange tie with the blue stripes, Des Cheshire seems a plausible psychopath, someone who really might commit genuine murder onstage just to enjoy the ensuing drama as it plays out. Relentlessly serene, perhaps effete and condescending, with his horn-rimmed eyeglasses glinting as his hands rest lightly on the strip of moulding that tops the sweat-smeared Plexiglas of the prisoner's dock, he smiles his Cheshire grin at the judge, to no particular effect.

"These two men were intimately linked for three decades, ladies and gentlemen, in what Mr. Cheshire had come to call holy deadlock. You will hear, in fact, that they even shared girlfriends." Pepino nods at the jurors sharply. "Yes, success had brought them wine and song, but also women — *babes*, in fact," Pepino can't help grimacing with distaste, "models, starlets, celebrity singers, barflies, beautiful women inaccessible to the average working Joe." The young prosecutor manages to flash a tight-lipped smile at three of the five men on the panel, the three who sit thigh to thigh. "The Crown will show that Mr. Wonder and Mr. Cheshire sometimes dated the same lovely ladies, competing for their affection. Their competition with each other, in other words, knew no boundaries. You will see that Mr. Cheshire presents, to use the psychiatric jargon, he presents as a friendly, joking, even intellectual man. But we will provide ample evidence, members of the jury, that this easy-going personality was eaten away by bitterness.

Greed and jealousy — male menopause, if you like — finally caused him to snap, in our respectful submission. One day, after some thirty years of working and touring with Billy Wonder, Des Cheshire realized that his salad days were just a memory and he was still playing second fiddle, or second saxophone, to a lesser musician. In late middle age, chafing under the terms of that one-sided contract and watching Mr. Wonder get all the credit and many of the women, well, Mr. Cheshire finally just lost it. Who wouldn't? you might even ask yourselves. In certain situations, none of us is a saint. I have thought that more than once as I have worked on this case. I have thought that there is a monster that lurks in the human heart, ladies and gentlemen, just waiting to be poked at one time too many. And before the end of this trial, the Crown will show you that monster's face, the monster that brought Mr. Cheshire to kill Mr. Wonder in rather spectacular and bitter circumstances: the green-eyed monster, as the poets call it, of jealousy."

Pepino calls the police evidence first, establishing that Wonder probably died between five and six p.m., of ligature strangulation.

"By ligature strangulation, you mean what?" she asks the forensic pathologist, Dr. Austin Rowse, of the Centre for Forensic Sciences in Toronto.

"Well, it seemed that someone had fashioned a garrotte, a wire with sticks, which the police found around the victim's neck." Rowse has a heavy Scottish brogue that makes it all sound like a bit of a lark.

"Yes, sir. So they have told us. In other words, he was strangled?"

"Well, generally, if you're using such a weapon, you would approach the victim from behind. So it was strangulation with that twist, pun seriously intended." The witness asks the clerk for Exhibit Three, the homemade garrotte, as a visual aid. "Coming over the top of his head you violently thrust the wire around the throat and pull him toward you, like this. At the same time, you twist the wire on the stick so as to asphyxiate him. It can also stop the blood flow in the jugulars, here at the side of the neck, rendering the victim unconscious before death, and making it simpler to strangle him. And in this case there were two sticks, as you can see, which made the deed even easier, I would think — two drumsticks affixed to a guitar string, like handles, on the heaviest string, the sixth one. It's a very efficient method, almost bound to kill."

"So you could do it fairly quickly, without that much ruckus?"

"Unless the victim was unusually strong, yes. If you took him by surprise, it wouldn't take long, or necessarily cause a commotion."

Pepino asks Dr. Rowse to demonstrate on her colleague, the somewhat startled lead prosecutor, Gordon Mortimer. The latter struggles to his middle-aged feet and stations his three hundred-odd pounds before the jury box, his ill-fitting robe reeking of cigarette smoke and dotted with holes from dropped ashes, his tabs, fat hands, and grey goatee stained brown with nicotine. The pathologist toddles up to Gordie from the witness stand with Exhibit Three. When he pulls gently back on the senior Crown's throat, Mortimer makes a meal of gurgling and falling against Rowse, so that the two of them topple to the floor, grunting and shouting and generally causing at least a minor ruckus. I resist the urge to flee the trial in a skittering panic, though it requires all the caginess of my own middle age. Pepino and the stenographer rush over to help the men up, but Gaunt is hypnotized by the demo, until Nadia Hussein, sitting behind him at the bar, punches him hard in the shoulder. He stands uncertainly and glances back at his insolent junior, rubbing his arm. Justice Honey glowers at him, snuffling, "You had something to add to the, er, demonstration, Mr. Gaunt?"

Gaunt snaps his head toward the bench as though he's been slapped from that direction. "Something to add, Your Honour?" Eventually he figures out why he's on his hind legs. "Yes, well, simply that perhaps Ms. Pepino should save her melodramatics for the Law Society's amateur theatre group. Outside of court time. It's inflammatory. Highly prejudicial to our case." He does not have a barrister's voice. In fact, his speech is reminiscent of the pained honk of the Canada goose.

"Well, I think the jury understands that this was a mere demonstration, Mr. Gaunt. Is that not so, members of the jury? A simple demonstration to show how you use this lethal little gadget, this garrotte, in general?" Justice Honey gives his best imitation of a benevolent smile, and several of the jurors nod and smile in reply. He in turn nods at the witness, who smiles and nods agreeably back. "No harm done, then, Doctor?" The judge's smile fades as he looks back down at Gaunt, and snuffles, "Personally, I found it rather instructive. Didn't you Mr. Gaunt? Someone could get hurt with these things."

Gaunt bows slightly and falls into his seat with his eyes closed — which is all the more unfortunate considering that Pepino has sat down and everyone in the room is staring at Gaunt, awaiting his cross-examination of pathologist Rowse. Nadia Hussein hits him again and he at last regains his feet, blinking.

"Des Cheshire doesn't play the drums, does he, Dr. Rowse?" Gaunt begins.

Pepino doesn't bother to stand. "The witness can't possibly know that for certain, Your Honour."

"Next question, Mr. Gaunt," Justice Honey rules, suddenly bored.

"Did you find any fingerprints on the drumsticks, Dr. Rowse?"

"Well, we found Mr. Denver's. Terry Denver is the drummer for Mr. Wonder's group, so that was to be expected. Apparently they were his drumsticks."

"Please stick to answering the question, doctor," the judge grumbles. "They might have been Mr. Denver's, they might not have been. We haven't heard evidence on that."

"The point is, Dr. Rowse, that Mr. Cheshire's prints weren't on the sticks, were they?"

"No, I don't believe they were."

"And you told us that killing someone with this gadget, as His Honour calls it, this garrotte, it's fairly easy to do?

"Easier than other methods of manual strangulation, certainly, such as using your bare hands, say, or a rope without the sticks. That is what I meant when I distinguished it from strangulation manually."

"So a woman could do it to a man?"

"Certainly, if she were tall enough in relation to the victim."

"Ah, but what if the victim were seated at a piano?"

Rowse smiles, conceding the point. "Fair enough, Mr. Gaunt. Then there likely would be no problem, for a woman of average capabilities."

"Those are my questions, Your Honour."

The judge looks up amazed, but also almost admiringly at defence counsel. "That's it, Mr. Gaunt?" Justice Honey smiles yet more broadly, revealing that such a gesture is riskier for the old curmudgeon than we had understood, given how loose his upper denture seems to be. Biting his false teeth back into place, he says, "Then perhaps this would be a good time to take lunch. Two-ten p.m., then, ladies and gentlemen."

It is ten after eleven in the morning.

CHAPTER 11

Oh, That Mack He's Back in Town

Obviously I cannot stay holed up behind the divan in Justice Mariner's chambers forever. Hunger, boredom, and yes, the ageing lion's wanderlust drive me back out the Hall's northeast doorway into the blustery and semi-mean streets of downtown Toronto. Without really thinking about it, I make my way — peripatetically, stopping at a couple of trash baskets here in New City Hall's parkette, there at the hot dog stand, there again near the skating rink, then bounding across Bay onto Albert with the bureaucrats and sales associates and law clerks on their coffee breaks, having a nosey at the police van that has carried the morning's batch of prisoners to bail and arraignment courts at Old City Hall — until I fetch up three or so blocks later at the garbage bins behind the Eaton Centre. Here, of course, resides the vagrant's smorgasbord, dependably overflowing with every sort of organic compound imaginable (never mind the children and other innocent mammals starving in Africa) — all the discards you can eat, neatly preserved in sheer black plastic, conveniently removable at dinner time with a couple of swipes of the paw. Sometimes you just about need a reservation, of course, given the city's teeming homeless of every species, not all of them willing to share nature's bounty, either. But just now all is peaceable and I have got nicely stuck into the disposable parts of yesterday's seafood marinara special at Just For the Halibut, Eaton Centre Level III, Queen Street entrance. The discarded mussel and lobster bits have my particular attention, lubricated as they are with what is either garlic butter or twenty-weight motor oil, I can't really tell for sure amid the general tumult and reek of the alley. That becomes moot, in any event, when suddenly my own trials resume, and ruin my appetite thoroughly.

Sensing a bit of shadow and movement, I glance up in mid-mastication to see Tantôt sneering down at me from the lip of an industrial cast-iron garbage bin. From that perspective, some three metres above, he looks all fang and claw. "Would you like flies with that?" he jeers. A bit of shrimp tail lolling sideways over my lower lip, I look left to see one of his enforcers trotting toward me, all dilated pupils and galvanized muscle, his bristling tail carried low; ditto, naturally, to the right. Keeping my cool, I leap and clamber (no, in midlife my shocks and springs ain't what they used to be) onto the lid of a nearby recycling bin, positioning myself at the midpoint of the equilateral triangle formed by my youthful would-be assailants. My not quite catlike acrobatics cause a wine bottle to fall from the bin and crash amid the rest of the over-flowing detritus on the asphalt, and the shattering glass is enough to give flinch and pause to the thugs below. In fact the thug stage-right performs one of those four-footed pogo-stick cat-leaps a metre straight in the air. Perhaps it's just nerves, but his panic attack strikes me as hilarious, calming me in spite of myself. *Fight or flight; flight or fight.* The diversion gives me the chance to work the shrimp tail off my tongue and begin my final address to the court — quite literally the *tri*-bunal — as it picks its treble-fanged way on twelve razored feet through the Has-being wasteland that is life on planet Earth, circa 2005.

Gentlemen of the jury, for better or worse nature has made us jealous — jealous of our space and everything that it represents for us: our sustenance, our shelter, our very survival. The place where we eat, sleep, and fornicate. It is our very selves, and the law of nature, the bio-logic, permits us to defend it with that degree of violence necessary to repel the particular threat. This is what both the law of nature and Has-being law describe as self-defence. In this very alleyway, as we try to make our living, we feel the daily tension of it in our sinew and bones. In fact, we feel it quite intensely just now, I would suggest. And this urge to defend our shelter and sustenance, our very being, becomes even more pronounced as we reach midlife, when we are more keenly aware of our own mortality. We hear time's winged chariot, as the poet says, hurrying near, while yonder, all before us lie deserts of vast eter-nity. [It has its practical applications, somnolently browsing the Norton anthologies of literature does, over His Lordship's shoulder from the back of that armchair.] *And where once we laughed and batted such winged creatures out of the air, we lack our former strength and will. All is mortality.*

We find ourselves old lions defending our turf with fading powers, fronted by young lions, you up-and-comers anxious to make your own mark, and rightly so, in the brave new world. And just as in human law, all of us are permitted to use only that degree of force sufficient to repel obstacles and threats to our getting on. Otherwise, there would be so many deaths among toms that our species would be decimated and, finally, self-annihilated. Just as human law "does not intend absurd results" (or so have I read in Has-being books on statutory interpretation), so does the law of nature abhor counter-productive self-defence strategies. However, sometimes, through inadvertence, fate intervenes, and even restrained and reasonable self-defence results in death.

I pause here to muse with momentary calm that Gaunt might like to use this argument in defence of Desmond Cheshire.

And yes, nature has its purpose in weakening us as we age, resist it though we might, like a dying star. When death comes to an assailant who happens to be old, weak, and half-mad with dementia — to one who, indeed, does not seem to comprehend that his time is past — one can say that the law of nature actually intends his death. He is, as the Has-beings say, over the hill. For he has served his term and purpose, fading from the horizon of progress. Nature declares that it is time for him to clear the path. That, I respectfully submit, is why our good friend and esteemed colleague, Baudelaire, late of Cabbagetown and more recently of Yorkville Village, has passed on to live in memory. He has, indeed, made way for your good selves. And that is why his death was lawful, or as the Has-beings sometimes say, justifiable homicide. And so do we gather together here today in his memory. Please, then, friends and colleagues, join me in a moment of silent remembrance.

Of course, blasted out of their minds on adolescent hormones (as per usual) and spoiling for a fight, my opponents remain deaf to the mature voice of reason. Perhaps it is just the gusting winds blowing all the garbage about, but Tantôt even seems to have donned a black cap, or at least a stained plastic bag that says *Haymishe Bagel* on it, to pronounce sentence of death against me. He thunks down blindly onto the lid beside me, the bag snagged on his snout as he sends yet more bottles and cans crashing to the pavement, causing his hench-felines to leap reflexively toward us in a panic of self-preservation. They are all three upon me, and upon themselves, in an orgy of hysterical violence, and I am about to be shredded for the dining pleasure of the evening's early-bird crows or nightfall's first racoons and stray dogs. Then a yowl stops us all ice-cold.

Ça suffit! You have just heard zis old tom tell it you. What is the point, tearing each other into the pieces? It is the voice of one who has tongued gasoline at midnight from the filling station court-yards on Spadina and Queen, to slake his dogday thirst; one whose hunger has caused him to suck the marrow from a squirrel's ribs as it lay crushed and picked over by ravens in the gutter of Lakeshore Boulevard, the traffic hurtling by at one hundred twenty klicks an hour just inches away. It is, of course, the voice of that old son of a queen, Baudelaire.

Yes, sure enough, he says, *it is I. You t'ink a simple bump on zuh 'ead, zat's enough to get you rid from me,* mes vieux? *Bon, t'ink again,* mes amis, *you là. I live to fight another time. Zuh King is alive. God save zuh King. And zat said, who is being zuh first contender? Allons-y! Claws up and out!*

Baudelaire glances from one to the other of us, daring a challenge. Were they not scared witless, the would-be contenders and pretenders and avengers would realize that they now lack a motive to visit capital punishment on Yours Wrongfully Indicted. *Directed verdict of not-guilty of manslaughter and any lesser, included offence.* The four of us younger toms stand atop the recycling bin gaping at the resurrected demi-god below, until we recover our wits just enough to flee as quickly as our little legs will carry us, in all four directions of the compass.

CHAPTER 12

When Gianna Loved Me

Nadia Hussein and I sit at His Lordship's desk — or, rather, *on* his desk, in my case — consulting the *Canadian Oxford Dictionary*. Hussein runs the cap of her pen (its top masticated on separate occasions by both of us) down the page headlined **Gorno-Altaisk / gord** until she hits **Goth**, definition 3b: "a member of a subculture favouring black clothing, white and black makeup, metal jewellery, and goth music." Goth music, definition 3a says, is a form of punk rock that frequently features "apocalyptic or mystical lyrics."

This doesn't provide us any particular help in preparing our cross-examination of Kitten Ravenscroft, but it gives you a fair idea of the impression she makes as she stands in the witness box with her head bowed: solemn, reluctant, distant, studiously mystical (or at least spectral), costumed (as much as clothed) in a black shawl and floor-length, closely-pleated black dress with lace cuffs and bodice. Apocalypse now.

Examining her in-chief, Pepino is having none of it. A hand on her jutting hip as good as says, *Let's cut the crap, shall we, Missy?* Orally, and in short order, Pepino establishes that Ravenscroft was present at the Chicken Alley on the afternoon of the murder, but that she was away from the table on a washroom break in the early evening — yes, probably around five or so. Jersey had let her inside to wait for "her boyfriend," Billy Wonder. She heard Billy rehearsing from behind the curtain, but when she came back from the washroom, the stage had gone quiet. She assumed Billy had returned to his dressing room upstairs. Ravenscroft gives all this evidence with her chin nearly on her chest, her heavily-mascaraed eyes hooded. Both Pepino and Justice Honey admonish her several times to speak up so the jury can hear her.

It is late afternoon when Gaunt begins his cross-examination. "You've been in psychotherapy, haven't you, Ms. Ravenscroft?"

"Yes. Counselling, really. Motivational coaching. Visioning. Like many artists."

"But you're not really a professional, are you? Artist, I mean."

For the first time during her testimony, Ravenscroft looks up, fixing Gaunt with a witchy, hooded glare. "I'm between jobs, Mr. Gaunt."

Gaunt consults his notes, even though they contain nothing on this particular subject. "But, as far as singing goes, you haven't had *any* jobs, have you?"

Ravenscroft sniffs. "I have. Open stages. New Voices nights."

"But you haven't been paid for any of that, have you?"

"So that means I'm unprofessional?"

"And you were waiting for Billy Wonder in the club, you say?"

"Yes."

"Even though you're not especially interested in jazz?"

"Who says I'm not?" Ravenscroft turns to Justice Honey.

"Certainly not myself," the judge replies, wriggling his neck in his judicial collar.

"Well, you're, um, what is it, now?" Gaunt turns to his learned junior, Ms. Hussein, for assistance. "Ah, right. You're Goth, aren't you?"

"She's what, Mr. Gaunt?" the judge asks, wrinkling his ruddy nose so that it stands out on his face like an ugly little crocus bulb.

"Goth, Your Honour. A fan of hard rock music." Hussein hits Gaunt in the fanny with her notebook. Glaring at her, he takes her proffered research and reads the definitions from the *Canadian Oxford*.

"Make that punk rock, Your Honour."

"If you say so, Mr. Gaunt. I hope nothing much depends on it."

"It's just a stereotype," the witness complains, glancing anxiously at the judge. "Prejudice. I get it all the time, just like I seem to be getting it here, on all fronts."

"I apologize if I've stereotyped you, Ms. Ravenscroft. I'm just saying that you tell us you were waiting for Billy Wonder, but, well, he had no idea you were there, did he, in fact?"

"He was busy. Rehearsing. Warming up. Doing his sound check or whatever. Getting ready for the gig. He had to focus on that. But Mr. Doucette was going to tell him I was there. He promised me. Twice."

"It was up to Mr. Doucette to tell your 'boyfriend' you were there?"

The witness is silent, so Gaunt presses on. "I'm interested in those times you were away from your table that afternoon, Ms. Ravenscroft. Three times, you told the police. You've said to Ms. Pepino that you went to the washroom a couple of times. What about the other time?"

"Why, I went to let the cat out."

"Which cat was that?"

"Well, they had this cat there, the bar cat I guess. It was black, but it had these really distinctive markings on its chest. White. They looked something like those ribbon thingamies hanging down from your collar, there."

Gaunt smiles at the jury. "For the record, the witness is indicating my tabs. That would have been Amicus, I believe, Your Honour. The Chicken Alley cat. Amicus Curious, I call him."

"How enormously interesting, Mr. Gaunt," the judge says to the courtroom ceiling. "Not to say relevant to these proceedings. Rather like your rock music evidence, apparently."

"And you let him out, Ms. Ravenscroft. How come it doesn't say that in your witness statement to the police? That you opened the door for the cat?"

"Well, I guess I didn't think it was important." This seems to incite sniffing from the bench, allergic as the court is to irrelevancies. "The cat was kicking up a fuss at the back door, in the kitchen, so I let him out. And anyway, I went to the washroom right after, so in fact I did tell the police, more or less."

"That you just moseyed into the kitchen, like it was your own, and let the cat out the back?"

"I was trying to help, Mr. Gaunt. As I say, the cat was making a racket."

"But you felt comfortable going into the kitchen, yet not going onto the stage to see your so-called boyfriend, Mr. Wonder?"

"I've told you. Billy was busy. I've told you."

"Indeed, she has told him," Pepino objects.

Gaunt bows toward the assistant Crown and moves on. "And this was before your second bathroom break?"

"No, just before the first one. On my way, as it turned out. I went from the back door to the ladies' room." The witness glares again at Gaunt. "As long as I was up."

"And was the back door locked before you opened it for the cat?"

Kitten Ravenscroft groans softly, rocking back on her heels in the witness box, wrinkling her nose in unconscious imitation of the judge. "Yes, now that you mention it, I believe it was. There was a deadbolt on it, and I had to turn it."

"And did you re-lock it after you let Amicus the cat out?"

Ravenscroft rolls her eyes and shrugs. "I don't know, Mr. Gaunt. It's not something you put a lot of thought into."

"So there's a good chance you didn't lock it."

"Well, actually, I'm not one of those paranoid people who're always locking their doors. I leave my doors at home open all the time. Even at night, usually. And this was a business premises, where people are pretty well meant to come and go at will, aren't they?"

"And so the back door still would have been open while you were in the washroom."

"If I didn't lock it, obviously, yes, it would have been open."

"And you say you're not one of those paranoid types."

"No, sir. I have great faith in my fellow humans. Actually, I have a diploma in social work. The music came later. I'm a people person, really."

"Really? And so, as a Goth sociologist, you would be familiar with the term 'erotomania,' Ms. Ravenscroft?"

Pepino is back on her feet with her hand on her hip. "What does that have to do with this murder charge against Mr. Cheshire?"

Gaunt swallows, closing his eyes. "It has to do, Your Honour, with Ms. Ravenscroft's mental capacity and behaviour, not only as it applies to Mr. Wonder, the deceased, but also as it might affect her observations of these events, her credibility as a witness."

"I'm going to allow it, Ms. Pepino," Justice Honey rules. "At least until we see where he's going."

"Erotomania is another term for erotic paranoia," the witness says. "But it doesn't come up in social work, Mr. Gaunt. It's a psychiatric term. Erotomania is not a social phenomenon as such. Generally it's viewed as a mental illness, of the individual."

"And has been applied to you by your therapist."

Ravenscroft scoffs, her eyes flashing. "One therapist, who I no longer have anything to do with, if you must know. I stopped seeing him a long time ago. He was useless. Off in the head himself." She is waving her hands and swaying in the box. "A quack. A disaster. The only man I ever met who suffers from penis envy." The jury laughs at the old joke, oblivious that Ravenscroft has stolen it from Joy Almundy in another endearing reference to her beloved "Normal" Clapham. (To make full and fair disclosure, Almundy was several Brandy Alexanders to the wind at the time. And stealing jokes, stealing licks, that's showbiz, I guess, not an indictable offence.)

"A useless delusional quack disaster who's off his nut. Ever hear of the pot and the kettle, Ms. Ravenscroft?"

Before Pepino and Mortimer can howl, Justice Honey says, "That'll do, Mr. Gaunt."

"I apologize, Your Honour, and to you, as well, Ms. Ravenscroft. What I want to know, though, is do you always react so violently when you disagree with someone?"

"Your Honour . . . ," Pepino begins.

The judge reluctantly bestirs himself into his next higher level of chronic irritation. "I said that'll do, Mr. Gaunt."

"But it's true Dr. Hafner angered you, Ms. Ravenscroft, didn't he? Upset you because he used the term 'erotomania' to describe your propensity to fall madly, off-your-head in love with celebrities? Particularly musicians? Who don't actually share your amorous feelings?"

"This sounds a lot like hearsay to me." Pepino jumps up yet again.

"Your Honour, if Ms. Pepino would just refrain for ten seconds from interfering with my cross-examination," Gaunt turns and looks directly at his "friend," the hopeful (some say conspiratorial) term lawyers use for opposing counsel, "the cross-examination which I am entitled to undertake without these interruptions, in the interest of my client. . . ." Gaunt gasps in exasperation. "If she'd just stop trying to derail it to keep me from testing this witness's evidence, she would understand that I'm putting this matter to the witness, herself. I'm not relying on any medical records or whatever. It's not hearsay."

"Ms. Ravenscroft." Labouring for breath as he turns heavily toward the box, the judge can barely bring himself to look at the Goth witness. "Can you just tell us if you've had diagnoses of this disorder, diagnoses that you fall in love with these musicians or whatnot, as a matter, I don't know, as a matter of delusion, or of some pathology?"

Ravenscroft returns the judge's disfavour, keeping her angry stare fixed on counsel for the defence. "How would Dr. Hafner know that, Mr. Gaunt? I'd be interested to hear, as a matter of psychology *and* of sociology. How the *hell* would he know if someone loves me? Or, for that matter, how the hell would you know?"

"Language, Ms. Ravenscroft," the judge says, with a sidelong glance at the witness, then another at the bailiff, who takes the cue and moves closer to the box.

"What I'm trying to say, Ms. Ravenscroft," Gaunt continues his questions, "is that Billy Wonder didn't love you at all, did he? In fact, he thought you were a pest, a stalker, isn't that right? At one point he even got a restraining order against you, didn't he?"

The witness's face goes red right through her make-up so that she looks a little like a jack-o'-lantern. Her heavily shadowed eyes dart up at the judge as she pants out her answer. "Certain people turned him against me, yes, but he cared for me, very deeply. Our relationship had its ups and downs, but he wrote his songs for me, love songs. You know that, but you're just misleading the jury, Mr. Gaunt." The bailiff comes through the swinging gate and stands near the prosecution table. "That song, 'When Joanna Loved Me,' for instance. That was for me, that's my name in English. Joanna."

Gaunt scoffs, cocksure and genuinely amused. "But that's an old Robert Wells tune, isn't it, from before you were born?" As Gaunt has told Justice Mariner, he owns all of Des and Billy's recordings. He smirks sidewise at Hussein, gloating over the one fact missing from her research notebook. "Billy didn't write that, did he? Neither did Des Cheshire." Then another thought hits defence counsel. "And doesn't Gianna translate as Jean? Isn't the Italian equivalent of Joanna 'Giovanna'?"

"It was for *me*, Mr. Gaunt. It was for *me*. And Billy helped Des Cheshire write love songs for me, too." The witness begins crying and turns to the bench. "But other people tried to turn them against me, Your Honour. Both of them."

"In fact, Des Cheshire warned you to stay away from Billy, didn't he, Gianna? Which made you pretty angry at Des, too, didn't it?"

"Des was jealous. He wanted me for himself, and people were trying to come between all of us — me, Billy, and Des, too. The atmosphere was thick with jealousy like it was a fog or something. A *smog*." Kitten Ravenscroft scowls briefly through her tears at Almundy, who sits in the well of the court, enjoying the proceedings enormously. She would be nibbling away at popcorn with loads of butter, you would imagine, were it not forbidden. A man sitting next to her looks vaguely familiar, and equally entertained by the goings-on. I suddenly realize that it is Norman Clapham, minus his spectacles and with his hair now closely cropped, looking considerably younger and less weedy. I imagine this is Almundy's influence: the poor man is becoming a Frankenstein's monster. "People forced Des to warn me off — Joy, for instance, and Des's agent, Morgan Denny," Ravenscroft continues, "because they both loved me, Des and Billy did, and it was all very emotional and distracting. It was causing tensions in the group. We all found it so distracting, from our careers and all. But we loved each other, quite desperately." She smiles lovingly at the man in the prisoner's dock, who suddenly looks at the floor. "As artists and as, well, people. And other people were trying to come between us for their own reasons."

"And what reasons would those have been, Ms. Ravenscroft?"

The witness stops crying as she shifts in the box, but she pulls at the lace collar of her black dress, looking anxiously here and there around the courtroom and then at the bailiff, nothing of the Goth so much as a cornered doe, panicked, angry, casting about between fight and flight. "I don't know," she shouts. She swallows hard and looks at the judge. "I don't know. Like I said, jealousy, I guess. Jealousy." The anger leaves Kitten Ravenscroft's face and she grows tearful again. She cocks her head at Gaunt and repeats, "Jealousy." She makes a snocking sound in the back of her throat and her knees seem to buckle as she flashes a pleading glance at Gaunt, then a look of abject supplication at the bench. She gasps, then whispers: "I'm afraid I don't feel very well. I need some air. I can't breathe." Her hand flies to her breast. "I can't breathe." Ravenscroft flees the stand, but Justice Honey holds up a hand at the bailiff, signalling that he should let the witness go.

"She's under subpoena, I take it?" the judge asks Mortimer, who nods. As Ravenscroft bangs out the door, Justice Honey suggests, "You might just want to send someone around later to remind her." Then he checks his watch. "Well." Justice Honey gazes at the floor between the counsel tables, pursing his thin lips. "Shall we say tomorrow morning, then, Mr. Gaunt, to resume your examination of our absconding witness, alleged Muse to the giants of jazz?"

CHAPTER 13

The Lady Is a Tramp!

"Well, I can ask the judge to strike her evidence," Pepino says. From her desk nearby in Courtroom 4–8, Justice Honey's clerk repeatedly snaps the rubber band on the stack of paper before her, scowling at Gaunt as she and the assistant Crown await his answer.

"You wish," Gaunt honks, trying to scoff, but losing his balance instead, so that he crashes into the oak bar behind him.

"Counsel," the clerk says in disgust. "We've got to bring the jury in. It's twenty after."

"But she hasn't produced her witness," Gaunt whines. "The kitten's done a moonlight flit, in the middle of my cross — my very productive cross, I might add."

"Tell you what," Pepino says. "You let me call Almundy for the limited purpose of a reply to your cross-exam so far on Ravenscroft. I won't take it any further than what you've asked Ravenscroft, just like I'd be limited in re-examination of her personally. Then you have a whole new cross-exam of Almundy as a whole new witness. Plus you get another crack at Ravenscroft, when we find her, and I can't touch her."

"Give me a minute," Gaunt says, as the clerk complains,

"Counsel!" Gaunt prevails on Pepino to lend him her cellphone and he comes back to his seat near Nadia Hussein and phones Justice Mariner. Unfortunately, His Lordship is already in court himself.

"Look, what do we have to lose?" Hussein asks. "We can get Almundy to confirm that Ravenscroft's a nutbar. And at the same time she'll show that she's a nasty little tart herself. Small, but mean and angry. Raise a suspicion in the jury's mind that either of them could've done it."

Gaunt casts a glance at the oblivious (and small but angry) Almundy, who smiles wetly at him, batting her beautiful eye-lashes. Until I met her, I was unaware that Has-beings really did that. "I don't trust either of them," Gaunt says. And, true enough, Almundy looks as though the popcorn butter wouldn't melt in her mouth. "My cross of Ravenscroft hurt them, and they're looking for payback."

"What do you mean, 'they'?"

"Almundy and Pepino, both."

Hussein shrugs. "What've we got to lose, Leland?"

Gaunt returns the phone to Pepino as the clerk leads Justice Honey to the bench. Pepino informs him that the witness Ravenscroft seems genuinely to have absconded.

"Has anybody tried to contact her, Ms. Pepino?"

"I've had my office phone the bed-and-breakfast where she's staying, Your Honour. No luck."

"Madam clerk," the judge orders, "bench warrant to go for the arrest of Ms. Ravenscroft as a material witness. And get it to the police this morning, so we might have the pleasure of Ms. Ravenscroft's attendance after lunch."

"Meanwhile, Your Honour," Pepino continues, "my friend has agreed that I might call a witness who is not on the Crown's disclosure list, to fill in the holes left by Ms. Ravenscroft, as it were. The Crown calls Ms. Joy Almundy."

Suddenly Almundy no longer looks like she has any appetite for popcorn or Junior Mints. "But I don't have anything to say," she says very loudly, looking around her, and particularly at the new Norman Clapham sitting beside her. To her further chagrin, the new Normal merely smiles and shrugs, much as the old Norman Clapham would have done.

The bailiff leads the jury to its seats and the judge explains that as Ms. Ravenscroft is currently unavailable, the trial will proceed with the Crown's next witness. As Almundy prances angrily to the witness box in her stiletto heels, it's clear she's actually enjoying herself — relishing her own anger and being on stage with it. She's never "off," as they say in show business. After establishing that she is a professional singer of some international experience, Pepino asks her, "You were here yesterday during Ms. Ravenscroft's evidence?"

"Yes, if that's what you call it."

"What do you mean by that?"

"Well, really. Was that evidence or was that the evaporating witch scene from *The Wizard of Oz*? Testimony or performance?"

Gaunt stands. "Your Honour, that is a matter for the jury. Obviously, Ms. Ravenscroft is a woman with problems, and it is not for the witness to ridicule her."

"Move on, please, Madam Crown," Justice Honey rules.

"Were you previously acquainted with Ms. Ravenscroft, Ms. Almundy?"

"I've seen her hanging around the clubs. She followed Billy around a lot, or tried to. And I was in a voice class with her, when she came out to L.A. where Billy had a house. Uninvited, by the way. Flew all the way in from Columbus without so much as a by your leave. I tried to become friends with her, anyway, and to give her some professional advice before she made a bigger fool of herself. We figured maybe that way she'd get the message and leave us alone." Almundy pauses with a short, humourless laugh. "But she didn't appreciate it. She really was wasting her money *and* time, in my opinion, but she didn't want to hear it. When I levelled with her, diplomatically, of course . . ."

"Of course," Gaunt mutters from his counsel table, nodding at no one in particular, widening his eyes just a little for the jury's benefit.

". . . it just made her that much more determined to do the opposite. She's funny that way, as the song says. Contrary."

"You were with Mr. Wonder at that period?" Pepino asks. "As his girlfriend?"

"I wouldn't go that far."

Gaunt stands again. "Your Honour, our understanding is that Ms. Almundy goes that far pretty often. Our understanding is that she was in residence with Mr. Wonder, shall we say."

"Hey, jawbone," Pepino shouts, turning to defence counsel, and sharing a sneer at him with Almundy, "save it for your cross."

"That'll do, both of you," Justice Honey snuffles.

"Your Honour, the point is," Gaunt says, "my friend is going too far, here, herself. Ms. Pepino and I agreed that she would call this witness simply in reply to my unfinished cross-examination of Ms. Ravenscroft, and in return my friend would give me full latitude in cross-examining Ms. Almundy."

The judge watches his finger draw circles on the bench as he says, "Whatever Ms. Pepino told you, Mr. Gaunt, this is a trial in a law court, and the purpose of a trial is to get at the truth. You permitted her to call this witness without first providing you a willsay, so now you must live with whatever Ms. Almundy tells us, within the bounds of admissible evidence. Please continue, Ms. Pepino."

"We were dating, Billy and I, off and on," Almundy says, eagerly pre-empting Pepino.

"So it was not an exclusive relationship?"

Almundy smirks at the assistant Crown. "Exclusive relationship? I find that sort of thing cramps one's style. Don't you, Ms. Pepino?"

Pepino shows her teeth. "You also dated Mr. Cheshire?"

"Your Honour," Gaunt says, without bothering to rise, "same objection."

"Your Honour," Pepino replies, "it's relevant as a reply to Ms. Ravenscroft's allegations about people being jealous of her and Mr. Wonder. It's relevant as to the, I don't know, the dating rituals? . . . among these people. I don't know what to call it. The easy-come, easy-go atmosphere, which my friend himself has raised."

"Yes, Ms. Pepino. 'Dating patterns,' is maybe how we can put it. I guess we don't want to call it bed-hopping, do we?" The judge throws a lubricious look at the jurors, who stare back poker-faced, saving their candour for the jury room.

"Oh, for God's sake," Almundy says. "I went out a couple of times with Des, yes, for a laugh. Who didn't?"

"So it was accepted that you would all sort of go out with one another, as friends and whatever."

"She's leading, Your Honour," Gaunt observes, but Almundy answers anyway, and Justice Honey does not intervene.

"Of course, Ms. Pepino. We're musicians. We're out all night, almost every night, in clubs and bars. It's what we do. As friends. We party. We hang out. It's part of the job. Sex, I don't particularly regret to say, sex hardly ever comes into it. It's by the way. I mean, we're all just, you know, . . . too bloody tired. You know? And usually too blasted." Almundy favours the jury with a lustrous smile as they laugh appreciatively.

"So there was no reason for you to be jealous of Ms. Ravenscroft?"

"You must be joking."

"That's a no, as in, there was no reason for jealousy, at least in respect of Ms. Ravenscroft?"

"That's a definitely, absolutely not, Ms. Pepino."

"And no reason for her to be jealous of you?"

"There was no reason for any jealousy at all. First, Gianna wasn't really part of the scene. We're talking successful professional musicians here. I mean, if anyone . . ." The witness suddenly looks rattled, caught out by her own sharp tongue. "I mean, if anyone should be jealous, I suppose, I guess it would have to do with Gianna and my *current* boyfriend."

"Your current boyfriend?" Pepino says, less confidently than is her wont. "I thought . . ."

"Well, I mean, a man I'm currently seeing, okay? Jeez. Who's on trial here, anyway?" Almundy casts a skeptical look out at the well of the court, where Clapham seems correspondingly amazed. "This current . . . *friend* is always harassing me about Gianna — asking what she's like, telling me how she seems so mysterious and sad and lonely and helpless. A damsel in distress. She has that curious effect on men, I've noticed. She creeps around" — Almundy demonstrates, to the extent that the confines of the witness box permit — "all in black, like Death in a garter belt and black silk hose, silent as the grave. Calls herself Kitten, like some, you know, like some *escort*, some callgirl. So they want to know what she must be like, with her gothic sex-and-death schtick. I think they imagine she must be really hot in the sack or something. Volcanic." Almundy snorts. "Boys will have their little fantasies, won't they, Ms. Pepino?" Regaining her confidence, Almundy smiles at the jurors again as several — including those three apparently suggestible men — grin, shuffle, and return her more than amicable gaze.

"So you are in fact jealous of her?"

"Gimme a break. As I say, first of all, she doesn't even register on anybody's radar. Second, as I said, we're all just having a laugh. It's the enterprise we're in, Ms. Pepino." She does a little dance in the box, holding up her palms and making little circles with them as she hoarsely sings, "'That's enter-tain-ment!' If we were money-grubbing, sex mad, and jealous I guess we'd be . . . I don't know, lawyers?"

The jury laughs again, until the judge admonishes the witness, with a fawning smile, "Ms. Almundy. It is my particular job to annoy, if not insult, counsel. You keep this up, you'll have me in the unemployment line."

The witness smiles, thrusting her upper body at the fat old judge, cocking her head and doing that thing with her eyelashes again. "I'm terribly sorry, Your Honour. Maybe you could take up jazz piano instead."

Justice Honey seems to consider this seriously for a moment. "Probably not. It's too dangerous, judging from this case. But I'd have more time at my cottage on Georgian Bay, I suppose."

"Now there's a party spot, Your Honour."

"And the singing class, Ms. Almundy," Pepino interrupts sharply. "What did you think of Ms. Ravenscroft there?"

With exaggerated reluctance Almundy turns from the bench and shrugs. "Well, she has a passable light soprano, I suppose. Not really a jazz voice. It's airy-fairy, rather unsure of itself. If she were in her right mind, maybe she could do choral society thingamies. At her church or something. Operettas. That sort of thing." Almundy sniffs. "As a hobby."

"You say 'if she were in her right mind.' But you've never seen her act out — violently, I mean, strike out at you or anyone else?"

Almundy snorts again, and unconsciously makes fists of both petite, white hands as they rest on the railing of the witness box. "I'd like to see her try it." She sighs. "Look, my dear, she's just another one of those sad little groupies you get in the music business. There are thousands of them. At least a dozen for every musician. They just need to get a life, somehow, somewhere."

"You don't think she's dangerous — my *dear?*"

Almundy snorts yet again as Gaunt objects, "The witness is not a forensic psychiatrist, Your Honour."

"You're not frightened of her?" Pepino asks, and Almundy just rolls her eyes as Gaunt begins, "Your Honour. . . ."

"That's all right, Your Honour," Pepino says. "I'll turn the witness over to Mr. Gaunt's tender mercies now."

"You're a very demanding person, aren't you, Ms. Almundy?" Gaunt immediately asks, as he is already in face-off position.

"Isn't that the definition of a professional, Mr. Gaunt?"

"But you have a habit of taking it beyond the professional, don't you Ms. Almundy? Isn't it true that you date quite, well, quite carnivorously. Rapaciously, even. That you, to use the vernacular, go through men at quite a clip?"

"She's already explained that, Your Honour," Mortimer objects for the prosecution. "And personally I've never heard of the concept of carnivorous dating. Except for Valentine's Day at the steakhouse, I guess. Anyway, she's explained the socializing among her peers."

"She has," Justice Honey snuffles at his notepad.

Gaunt tries another tack with Almundy. "But you haven't told us that you're on rather a short fuse, have you Ms. Almundy? That you're quite notorious for walking off jobs if the conditions don't suit you? That you're very assertive with producers, booking agents, club owners, not to mention bandleaders and everybody else you encounter?"

"I don't see the relevance of this, Your Honour," Mortimer interjects. "Although it's quite a speech. And to support it, I assume Mr. Gaunt is prepared to call all of these producers, booking agents, clubowners, and bandleaders, and I guess everybody else Ms. Almundy encounters." In support of her leader, Pepino arches her eyebrows at counsel for the defence.

Justice Honey echoes the Crown, noticeably shaken about how this mass of evidence might interfere with his time at the cottage on Georgian Bay: "Relevance, Mr. Gaunt?"

Ignoring the interruption, Gaunt asks, "You don't suffer fools gladly, do you, Ms. Almundy?"

"Well." Joy Almundy has gone red, but she takes a beat, then recovers her pallor as she replies, "Let's just say I'm not feeling especially glad right now, Mr. Gaunt." She fixes Leland with a sparkling smile. Then, yes, she does that business with the eyelashes.

"Those are my questions," Gaunt says, sitting back down, looking grimly at his papers on the counsel table.

CHAPTER 14

I've Grown Accustomed to Her Face

At sea in the bad press over the Wonder murder, Jersey has given in to the two kids who want to hold a songathon at the Alley. Their "so-call-it big idea," as Jersey describes it just before the fun begins, is to chant "baby," or, more precisely, "baybeh," in a monotone (okay, the monotone isn't part of the idea, exactly, so much as it's what eventuates), as many times as possible, to the accompaniment of a hip-hop drum-machine beat and the repeated three-chord progression:

C C	*F F*	*G7 G7*
Baybeh.	*Baybeh.*	*Baybeh.*
C C	*F F*	*G7 G7*
Baybeh.	*Baybeh.*	*Baybeh.*

"Why these kids from Scarborough always want to talk like they're a Alabama sharecropper, don't ask me," Jersey says.

"Mah baybeh done left meh," Justice Mariner sings.

"Ah cain't get nuh satisfac-chun," Jersey responds.

"Though ah trahhed, and ah trahhed, and ah trahhed . . ."

The "kids" are, in any event, trying to get into the *Guinness Book of World Records* and the public is invited to the Alley to show their support over a few drinks, with ten percent of the proceeds slated for the Humane Society, in honour of Your Amicus Tabernae (friend, more or less, at this kind of bar, too). If they flub, like missing one baybeh or putting in a "pretty momma" or "my honey" / "mah honeh," that's it. They have to start over or give it right up. Some fool is actually recording the thing, not Cueball Finkelstein this time ("my regulars won't come near my place tonight," Jersey notes), but some old granola who claims he crashed John Lennon's honeymoon, that so-called "bed-in for peace" in Montreal, 1969.

"Everything's changed, hasn't it, Jers?" The Baybeh Marathon gears up, the audience thrusting beer mugs in the air and shouting along in hooligan unison while His Lordship and Jersey lean over the railing on the back steps overlooking the dark alleyway, where I, too, have taken refuge. "It used to be pure adrenaline — the music, the sex, the booze, but mostly the music, eh, in the perfumed air and the perfect black night? Now, it's, I don't know . . . the quality of the night isn't what it was, you know? It's all show — strapless linen slit up to the ying-yang or hanging off their hips, naïve little administrative assistants snorting lines of coke in the toilets, those gun-metal sport utes roaring out of the underground parking lot on Cumberland. It's all, I don't know, compromised, bought and paid for. Reflexive self-assertion, the new epidemic, everything for show. Oprahfication. The night's not perfect any more, is it, Jers? Everything's changed."

About half an hour later, Jersey will ask Sylvie and College, the math major from the U of T who sometimes waits the Alley's tables these days, to watch the place while he drives around the city for an hour or so in his '68 Lincoln, just repainted baby blue with ivory trim. A couple of people will nearly drive off the road when they see the old barkeep caterwauling and gesticulating with the top down, throwing his hands up in the air like a madman, leaving the wheel to its own devices as he sails down Bay Street with no one sitting in the passenger seat or in the back. For now, however, out behind his funky little bar, he simply nods and says, "That's the truth, Briefs. Everything's changed. It sure enough has."

⌒◯◯⌒

"We've got a problem finishing up your cross on Ravenscroft." Pepino approaches Gaunt as soon as he enters the courtroom that afternoon. She tries moderately hard not to smirk, waggling a pencil between her fingers at high speed, as though she holds captive a hummingbird bloated on her juicy news.

"She's absconded, right?" Gaunt cocks that double-joined jaw. "Left town? Left the country?"

"Well, actually, you might say she's left the building." Pepino tries less hard not to smirk.

"Duh-uh! I know she's not *here*, Melody." Gaunt gawks dramatically around the room, now occupied mostly by reporters from the international press. "Otherwise, we'd just put her back in the box."

"No, Leland. Listen, sweetie." Pepino's not altogether merciless smile breaks free, briefly. "You know how they say Elvis has left the building? Well, so has Gianna a.k.a Kitten Ravenscroft."

Gaunt shakes his head and shrugs at Nadia Hussein as she

clucks in disgust. "She means the kitten's dead, Leland." The women roll their eyes at each other.

"Deceased," Pepino says.

"Had the biscuit," Hussein says.

"Bought the farm," a reporter sitting just behind Gaunt adds, never mind that he is from Denmark.

"Yes, all right," Gaunt says, lowering his voice and moving away from the bar with his learned junior and junior counsel for the Crown. "I might be thick, but I'm not deaf."

"They think it's suicide," Pepino explains.

"Oh, Jesus," Gaunt says. "Really, Mel? Jesus. I feel terrible. I mean, I didn't intend to send her over the edge. I was only doing my job, guys."

Pepino looks at him as though he, too, is out of his mind. "Crikey, Lee. Get a grip. Your cross was really great, I'm sure, but I doubt very much that you killed her. Mind you, I can consult with Gordie, if you want, about getting you charged with manslaughter."

Hesitantly, Hussein puts a hand on Gaunt's shoulder. "You didn't push her, Leland. She jumped. She'd been on the ledge for a long time, you know." Gaunt does not look much comforted.

"Actually, the interesting thing is," Pepino says, eyebrows up, "she died by ligature strangulation. Garrotting, to be precise." She does a credible job of sounding quite blasé.

Gaunt stares open-mouthed, Hussein wide-eyed.

"No shit. According to my guy . . ."

"Your guy?" Gaunt asks, dazed.

"The constable who went to arrest her for not showing up this morning. At the B and B where she was staying, in that old sorority house on Madison Ave. He found her, fully clothed, on her stomach in her bed, in her famously unlocked room. She'd used the E string from her guitar, just like what happened with Billy Wonder. Knotted it onto a big fountain pen, apparently. Twisted it around her own neck."

"You can do that?"

"The forensic guys say yes. They hadn't seen it before, but it's not unknown. Once you've twisted it with the stick or whatever, the pressure stays on, see, and it takes you out, eventually. It's rare, but it happens, sometimes as a sort of sexual thing, they said. Masturbatory, I guess." Pepino shivers in unconvincing disgust. "Extra rush at climax, apparently. Autoerotic asphyxia, it's called. Dying for love. Or self-love." The assistant Crown shrugs and grimaces.

"So maybe she did it for . . . for pleasure?" Gaunt asks, with mingled dread and hope.

"Well, I doubt it, actually," Pepino brings him crashing back down. "My guess is, she was just screwed up generally and she actually wanted to, you know, *die*."

"Otherwise she was one weird, oversexed lady," Hussein says, crinkle-nosed herself. "Autoerotic paranoia. Autoerotic asphyxia. Self-love, self-loathe, take your pick, place your bets."

Gaunt waves at his colleagues and at the room in general as he sinks into his seat at the counsel table. "Please. I don't need to know any more right now. Please. No more."

"But there'll have to be an inquest, of course," Pepino says to Hussein. "And here's something to make you feel better, Lee." She turns back to senior counsel. "They found her journal. As soon as the forensics are done with it and I get it photocopied, we'll disclose it to you. This afternoon, tomorrow at the latest. A real page-turner, I betcha." Pepino clicks her tongue.

"Yeah, great," Gaunt replies as Pepino moves away to speak to Justice Honey's clerk. "I won't be able to put it down, I'm sure."

Hussein watches until the assistant Crown is out of earshot, then she punches poor, miserable Gaunt in the shoulder again. "Hey, man. Don't you see? It's fantastic. Our best break yet."

"Damn it, Nadia, stop hitting me, will you?"

Hussein hits him again, harder. "This is a gift from the gods, Leland. I mean, may the poor loony rest in peace and all that, but . . ."

Massaging his shoulder, Gaunt looks up at her nonplussed. "Don't you see?" she asks. "We can move for a dismissal, or ask the judge to direct the jury to acquit. It looks like she did it to Wonder, too, no?"

"No, not necessarily, Nadia. As Melody says, it just confirms that she was a very disturbed young woman. But it's worth a shot, I suppose. I mean, we should run it by the judge."

Corkscrewing her mouth in thought, Nadia Hussein nods. "When he comes in to hear the big news, we'll move for a dismissal of the charge. Hit him with the old one-two, before he can think about it. I mean, Leland, a formal motion."

Gaunt looks unconvinced, but still rubbing his shoulder he gives in wearily. "Yes. All right. All right. Just stop hitting me, okay? And prepare a notice of motion to serve on Gordie."

᠙᠙᠙

From the start, Justice Honey appears to agree with counsel for the

Crown, who, for the purposes of Gaunt's motion for dismissal, is Gordie Mortimer, taking over from his "learned junior." "Number one," Mortimer says, or wheezes, his very person reeking of Rothman's king-size (the pong of it wafting several yards, and notably to where I lie under the clerk and stenographer's table), "the police believe it's suicide. There's no indication it has anything to do with the Wonder murder."

"But that's just it, Your Honour," Gaunt says, in the absence of the jury, naturally. "The police will want to reopen their investigation now into the Wonder *death*. To sort it all out. How this fits in."

"You're suggesting the Wonder murder is suicide, too, Mr. Gaunt?" Mortimer asks, putting an expression on for the judge that loudly mimes, *Can you believe this guy, Your Honour?* "He killed himself onstage?"

"No, but if the Ravenscroft death is suicide, that puts a whole new complexion on Mr. Wonder's unfortunate demise, in my respectful submission. It brings up several credible possibilities."

"So you're not suggesting there's a sudden rash of suicides with guitar strings, Mr. Gaunt?" Justice Honey asks the ceiling of Courtroom 4–8, rocking all the way back in his judicial chair.

"Well, not necessarily, sir, but there is a phenomenon that psychiatrists call *folie à deux*, I believe. You know, two people operating under the same mental illness or delusion."

"I think you're grasping at straws, Mr. Gaunt, if not G strings."

"I believe it was an E again, Your Honour," Gaunt points out.

"Any what again, Mr. Gaunt?"

"An E *string* again, Your Honour. Ms. Ravenscroft was strangled by an E string. The sixth string for a guitar. Just like Mr. Wonder."

"How very precise of you, Mr. Gaunt. So, you *are*, then, suggesting that there's a rash of suicide by E string?"

"That's not what we're hearing from the police, Your Honour," Mortimer repeats. "As our evidence has already shown, the force applied to Mr. Wonder, and the fact that the wire was slack when he was found, strongly suggest murder. Anyway, number two, even if we simply adjourn, well, if we delay this trial, it just keeps Mr. Cheshire in jeopardy that much longer, with these allegations hanging over his head. It compromises the trial. I mean, we might lose more witnesses. A lot of them have to travel to make their living or whatnot. Besides, I would have thought my friend would want to get this over with, for his client's sake."

"I do, Your Honour," Gaunt agrees. "And it'll be all done and dusted this very moment if my friend simply withdraws the charge, or Your Honour dismisses it. Apparently Ms. Ravenscroft was capable of doing this garrotting thing. And I believe it's fair to say that she was a very troubled young woman."

"And?" the judge asks.

"And, as our evidence has shown, several other people also had the motive and means, at least regarding Mr. Wonder. So I'm not talking about a rash of suicides, necessarily, although I suppose that's possible, too. What I'm asking is, given this new death by the same method, how can we continue to treat Mr. Cheshire as the prime suspect?"

"Prime perpetrator, you mean," Mortimer corrects.

"Mr. Gaunt," Justice Honey rules, "you know I can't order a dismissal on nothing more than your speculation that there might be some link between these two deaths. The woman clearly was unstable, and your whole cross-examination, I take it, was meant to show that her relationship with Wonder was illusory, if not lethal. But that works both ways. Maybe Wonder's murder just gave her ideas. Maybe she thought they'd finally be together in Heaven. There's nothing to show she killed him, or anybody killed her. On the other hand, the jury might take it all as confirmation of your cross-examination — that she was so unstable she *might* have killed Mr. Wonder. I don't see how proceeding with the trial can hurt you. You can still argue that her behaviour, and her death, raise a reasonable doubt concerning your client's role in all this."

"But, Your Honour, no one else except the owner and Ms. Ravenscroft was in the nightclub throughout the afternoon in question. So why continue with the trial of Mr. Cheshire, why put the jury to more trouble and clog up your own busy docket, when Ravenscroft was much more likely the killer?"

"That's up to the Crown and the police, Mr. Gaunt, not you and me. Anyway, people were in and out of that nightclub constantly. We've heard that. The staff. Your client, apparently. Mr. Profitt. Delivery people. Vagrants. There was Justice Mariner living upstairs."

"Surely you're not suggesting, Your Honour . . ." Actually, of course, Gaunt hoped the judge would tell the jury this very thing — that there was yet another suspect.

Justice Honey shrugs. "It's not my job to suggest, Mr. Gaunt. I'm just remarking that, look" — the judge leans forward and raises a finger — "we've got a bar with all the usual element it attracts, no? Creatures of the night. Not all of them have day jobs like us, Mr. Gaunt. So you've got all these comings and goings, plus there exist these upstairs premises and I don't know what else. Clearly there are a lot of places for people to secret themselves, people who belong there and people who don't. Comings and goings and doings, Mr. Gaunt. Drugs, sex, and rock and roll, I've heard tell."

"Not at the Chicken Alley, Your Honour. Mr. Doucette will not tolerate rock and roll on the premises." Apparently Leland is unaware of the Baybeh Marathon.

"All right, sex, drugs, and jazz then. Same difference. It's all the same cacophony."

"And we can't wait for the inquest into Ms. Ravenscroft's death, Your Honour," Mortimer says, nodding, before Gaunt can object to Justice Honey's apparent bias concerning jazz musicians. "It could be months from now. That would be unfair to the victim and to Mr. Cheshire both."

"Your interest in my client is very touching, Mr. Mortimer," Gaunt says, staring at the panelled wall behind Justice Honey.

Mortimer ignores him. "Witnesses die all the time, Your Honour." The court scowls and Mortimer catches himself. "Unfortunately, of course. But that doesn't mean justice stands still."

"If we stopped every time something like this happened," the judge agrees, "murderers would go free and the courts would be hopelessly backlogged. If the Crown wishes to proceed against some of these odds, Mr. Gaunt, well, I can't see how that prejudices your defence." He waves Gaunt off. "Your motion or application or whatever is, counsel, is dismissed. Let's bring in the jury, bailiff. Mr. Gaunt can put his alternative suspects to them. Counsel and I will have to discuss later how much, if any, of Ms. Ravenscroft's evidence can stay in."

CHAPTER 15

Gallows in Wonderland

November 12
Columbus, Ohio

 Gianna Ravenscroft Wonder Gianna Wonder G.
       Wonder
   Gianna & Billy Wonder g wonder
 Kitten in Wonderland G. I. Wonder? Gee I Wonder
   G.I. Wonder Whoskissingim—Now

<u>This journal is the property of Gianna Ravenscroft-Wonder</u>
Private! Keep out!!!

*so dr hafner says yes well thats alright gianna, fantasize being
mrs. billy wonder if you want to great let's just do it then go
through every single signature and cross it out with a big fat X.
We'll do it together. aversion therapy. stopping the delusional
thinking. you can do it gianna just apply yourself. the lightbulb
has to want to change. the other thing you can do gianna (hes
always adding to my todo list gee thanks gianna this gianna that)
is you can put a rubber band on your wrist and every time you*

have the thought that billy wonder loves you or hes sending you messages in his songs or that sort of thing you should snap it so it hurts a little. just a little not so as to injure yourself it isn't necessary. aversion therapy not self-abuse. no drugs necessary. i don't like using drugs gianna dr. hafner says. yeah right. so we start with the least interventionist and go on progressively until something works. alice in WONDERLAND *plays along of course nodding her head saying yessir yessir three bags full sir telling the words what to mean. they mean what she wants them to mean, which is alice in wonder. if we dont go along theyll say shes breached her restraining order keep away from billy or youre back inside some piss-stink cockroach motel jail or the shit-stink mental health centre with all the other maids and mugs in Bedlam where one pill makes you larger and one pill makes you small. of course as a scientist he doesnt understand passion dr. hafner doesnt i mean. how lovers communicate thru music. a glance across the room. over the radio. on their cds. on the tv. even by what they order from the menu at their hotel or the clubs. words of love. love is all around. love is in the air. music be the food of love . . .*

Mrs. Billy Wonder   Ms. Gianna Wonder
Mrs. G. Ravenscroft-Wonder
Kitten R. Wonder
Gianna in Wonderland

"It's really sad, isn't it, Nadia?" Justice Mariner asks, before sipping at his orange-and-cranberry juice on the rocks. It is late afternoon and he sits with his articled clerk and Leland Gaunt — and, oh, yes, Your Prodigal Son, of course — at a table in the

Alley, stirring his alcohol-free beverage with a miniature green plastic sabre. Although I am no longer a fugitive from injustice, we have been reunited in the face of imminent homelessness: Never mind that Jersey is less than ecstatic at Your Rover's return, the Wonder murder has brought the Alley to the furrow-browed attention of Her Majesty's fire marshal. Himself has served a squinty-eyed work order, threatening "closure of the said Licensed Premises in default of the aforementioned Work(s) having been performed and completed within 45 days of the issuance of the herein Order." Further, no person is permitted to "reside on or occupy the Premises as Resident." It says nothing of cats, but that don't make no never mind to Jersey, as he would put it himself.

"I mean, look at this," His Lordship says to Nadia Hussein as I thread among my professional colleagues, rubbing at their chins, sniffing at the pita bread and French fry crumbs on the table, accepting tributes, shrugging off rebuffs. "Recipes. Here's one for meatloaf, for God's sake, 'Billy's favourite.' How sad is that? Names for babies. Signing her name like she's married to Billy Wonder. Everybody thought she was so exotic, when her dreams were so, I don't know, banal. So, so . . ."

"Middle-class?" Gaunt says. "Like, what was that movie? *The Stepford Wives*, where the women are all brides of Frankenstein, pretending to be perfect homemakers until they massacre their husbands?"

"Bloody spooky," Hussein says. "Look at what she put in there the day after Billy was murdered."

The judge scoots me off the journal and flips forward in it. Several clippings having to do with Des Cheshire's arrest and trial scatter free of the binding. Presumably Kitten Ravenscroft never had time to paste them in place.

January 14

Toronto, Ontario

> *malice in wonderland*
> *to win the hand of queene alice*
> *the cheshire cat hath slain*
> *the king of wonderland.*
> *there is love enuf for all, saide she*
> *but they heeded her not at all.*
> *callous in wonderland*
> *phallus in wonderland — the Little Death,*
> *and its mortal progeny: jealous in wonderland*
> *my name is Death, o faire laydie,*
> *all kings and princes bow down unto me*
> *all kings and princes bow down unto me.*
> *wondrously the king is dead. long live the king of cats.*

Gianna Ravenscroft Cheshire   Gianna Cheshire G.
Cheshire
Gianna & Desmond Cheshire   g cheshire
Mrs. Desmond Cheshire   Ms. Gianna Cheshire
Mrs. G. Ravenscroft-Cheshire

tore this out of an obituary spread on billy and the band in downbeat magazine. (it was mr doucettes mag. but i'm sure he wont miss it. he gave it to me to look at. to pass the time he said heal the wound. he's a kind soul and very thoughtful of others. unlike some. keep cool but do not freeze, said the mayonnaise jar to little alice.)

Desisms: The Wit and Wisdom of That Old Cheshire Cat

db: Comparing you to luminaries such as Charlie Parker and Sonny Stitt, some people have called you the Great White Hope of the alto sax. Has that put a lot of pressure on you to meet some sort of standard?

DC: Not really, no. I mean, what standard could it be? We all have distinctive, individual styles. I just keep doing my own thing — what I call commotion recollected in tranquillity.

db: Yes, that's been widely quoted.

DC: It was just something I said in passing, really, to a reviewer who asked me how I would describe my style. I responded off the top of my head. Then it kept getting quoted like the Gospel — or at least like Wordsworth.

db: And then Miles Davis said that you needed more commotion and less tranquillity — that you were too white, your style being mostly air, light on its toes, non-committal, I think he put it. How do you respond to that?

DC: Well, as I say, I made that remark off the top of my head, and just like my receding hairline, I can't seem to get it back.

db: Recently, on Elvis in Wonderland, you and Billy delved into the popular idiom, playing songs by the Beatles, James Taylor, Britney Spears, Celine Dion. Was this purely for commercial reasons?

DC: It was purely for reasons that Billy wanted to go commercial. I mean, ironically, a lot of people think that Presley — or at least the marketing of popular music that grew up around him — they think it just about killed serious jazz. Made a lot of us has-beens overnight. So according to Billy it was sell out or sell up. He didn't think we could make it any more with straight-ahead jazz. He didn't think we were "relevant" in the new millennium, as he insisted on putting it. Change or die. Stay young. That sort of thing. Evil-lution, we called it behind his back. Maybe we should have said "Elvis-lution."

db: Word on the street was you resisted and Billy threatened to sue you for breach of contract.

DC *[silent for a long moment, then eyeing the interviewer with his trademark cagey smile]:* Well, the law does come into it. It was Justice Learned Hand, I think, who once said during a copyright infringement lawsuit, "While there are an enormous number of possible permutations of the musical notes of the scale, only a few are pleasing; and much fewer still suit the infantile demands of the popular ear." I suspect His Honour was a closet jazz fan.

Mr. and Mrs. Des Cheshire
Gianna Ravenscroft-Cheshire
Mrs. D. Cheshire

"Her philosophy seems to have been, life goes on," Hussein observes, her head still bowed as she shakes it sadly over Gianna Ravenscroft's journal.

The judge shakes his in reply, buzzing his lips softly.

"I'm not sure I'm wild about that 'the cheshire cat hath slain king wonderful' part," Gaunt says.

"Well, but she was obviously deranged," Justice Mariner says. "As evidence it won't have any weight. I mean, what does it mean?"

"On the other hand," Hussein says, "that clipping where Des attacks Billy as commercialized and infantile, well, it only adds fuel to the prosecution fire."

"Yes," Justice Mariner admits, "we should get a copy of the full article. Maybe Jersey's still got what's left of it. See if we can find something else in it more positive about their relationship."

"The thing is, Judge," Gaunt says, "time's running out on us. We're gonna have to call Des to testify in his own defence. We don't have anything else."

The judge looks glum. "Normally, a guy of his accomplishment and intelligence, I'd say no problem. But he's likely to come across as smart-alecky or bitter, and play straight into Pepino's hands. I mean, Nadia's right . . ."

Nadia's right, I can hear Gaunt mimic under his breath, from the side of his mouth.

". . . he can seem like one cold fish, this guy."

"But what option have we got, Judge?"

Justice Mariner is still listing the negatives. "And he's showy about his learning, like some pompous boulevardier. Very alienating for a jury. That whole 'look how cool and urbane I am' business. I mean, just imagine if he starts lecturing them on the history of garrotting, how he learned all about it in Spain or somewhere at this or that museum. Then we're dead in the water. As he said himself on the phone the other day, his next album might as well be called *Gallows in Wonderland*."

"But you know, Judge," Nadia Hussein, the other pedant for the defence pipes in, "it was actually featured in British law, the garrotte. Briefly, all right, but notoriously. It became so common at a certain time, as an instrument for robbing people in the streets, well, they passed an act specifically about it — permitting, you know, extremely stiff sentences for even attempting to do it."

"That's all very interesting, Nadia," Gaunt sneers, "but this isn't law school. It's real life, and the clock's ticking."

Justice Mariner raises a hand. "Hold your horses, Lee. We need any straw we can grasp just now. And the two of you cat-fighting at every pass doesn't get us anywhere. Go on, Nadia." Judiciously, I decide it's time for a snooze *underneath* the table.

Nadia reads from her notebook. "'*An Act for the Further Security of the Persons of Her Majesty's Subjects from Personal Violence.*' Apparently it amended earlier legislation concerning robbery, you know, by adding this business about 'being armed with any offensive weapon or instrument,' and choking, attempted choking. And the important thing is, it upped the penalties big time. You could get fifty strokes of the lash or what-ever, *fifty*, on top of imprisonment for life, on some convictions. 'In each case the court in its sentence shall specify the number of strokes to be inflicted and the instrument to be used.'"

This only makes His Lordship more miserable. "Oh, happy day. Judging would have been a real hoot in that era. Almost as fun as now, with people's lives hanging in the balance. Only, then, you got to wear a black cap, too, as you literally hanged people while they were off-balance."

Hussein remains cheerful despite the glum puns. "Well, but apparently this was truly what we would call general deterrence these days, like when you are passing sentence, Judge — without your black cap. This threat of whipping and such, it worked like a charm, I guess, because suddenly this rash of garrotting dried up, as fast as it began."

"There was a spate of these attacks before the flogging penalty?" the judge asks, pinching his chin with a desperate hand.

"Yes, sir, during this one season or so. That's apparently what stimulated the legislation. It came into force in July, and Bob was your uncle. No more robberies by the garrotte."

"And what year was this?"

"Oh, dear, I don't . . ." Nadia searches her notes. "Here it is, yes. I knew I had it. The legislation was proclaimed in July, 1863. So it was 1862 through 1863. Yes. Twenty-six and twenty-seven Victoria, as in Queen."[*]

"Eighteen sixty-three," the judge repeats, with a faraway look. "Mid-Victorian." Then suddenly he slaps the table hard with both hands, sending me skittering for the relative safety behind Jersey's bar. Justice Mariner leaps up and in his enthusiasm makes a rash mistake — and I am not talking about the empty glass he knocks to Jersey's freshly-mopped floor. He kisses Nadia Hussein full on the mouth. Gaunt looks on in mingled astonishment and depression, but His Lordship is oblivious, all rejuvenated hormones, Briefs Mariner as was, the bright young law student and busboy with all the world as his oyster. "That's it, you beautiful, exotic young creature," the judge shouts from the Jazz Age, as Jersey scowls at him from where he's trying to repair the coffee machine for the third time today. "You've got it! That's it!"

Hussein has gone quiet. She asks to be excused so that she can use the washroom. With a green-eyed look that is not quite loathing, Gaunt watches her go. His Lordship is still much too excited to notice anything amiss. "I don't think we'll have to call Des, after all, Lee" he says to Gaunt, rubbing his hands. "Pepino and Gordie won't get to lay a glove on him." The judge instructs Leland that, first thing in the morning, he is to get the Superior Court to issue a subpoena. "We have our star witness, Lee. Bloody hell, do we have our star witness!"

---

[*]The full citation in the British statute books is 26 and 27 Victoria, Chapter 44.

CHAPTER 16

Medley: The Way You Look Tonight / It Had to Be You

as it says on the hellmans mayonnaise jar, keep cool but dont freeze.

"That's all they found?" Gaunt asks Gordie Mortimer before court begins for the day. From my foxhole at the stenographer's sandals, I can see the two of them hunched over the counsel table Mortimer shares with the formidable Melody Pepino. Relegated to chambers again, courtesy of the fire marshal, I have made the daily commute to the courthouse through the underground tunnel. "They're telling us that's the whole of the note she left?" Gaunt gives Mortimer a baffled look. "I mean, it looks torn. See here?" He points to the jagged silhouette on the photocopy.

Mortimer shrugs. "The cops are still doing their forensics on the original. It's pretty crumpled up, apparently. Or creased. See, there, for example, you can notice it on the photocopy. Like she'd been carrying it around for awhile. But we're pretty sure that's the whole thing. It's raggedy, apparently, because she ripped it out of the diary she shlepped with her everywhere. Same paper. Matches a bit torn out, I'm told."

"What's this here?" Gaunt points to what must be a drawing under the last several words. "Eyeglasses?"

"Yeah. Horn-rim specs. Not unlike those worn by your client, you might like to note."

Gaunt shakes his head. "That girl was one sick puppy."

"Kitten, actually."

"Not funny, Gordie. Not even remotely."

"No offence meant, mate. You got to laugh to keep from crying, eh? But talk about your infamous last words. Bloody sad."

"Actually, that's no great mystery. She got them from the club owner. Via the refrigerator, as I understand it."

"This Doucette guy, you mean?"

"Yeah. Jersey Doucette. They used it as a kind of greeting. Flashed the peace sign and said, 'Keep cool but don't freeze.' It's in other parts of the diary, by the way. You should probably read the evidence, Gordie. You might begin to see you've got the wrong guy."

"Hey, man, keep cool but don't freeze!" Mortimer barks with laughter, so loudly that Gaunt winces and glances nervously around the courtroom. "Sounds like it could be the official motto of Canada."

"I guess it just stuck in her head. She and Doucette both mentioned it when we were interviewing witnesses, how it was their little joke. She said Doucette was the only one who treated her with any dignity."

"Poor sap," Gordie Mortimer says, patting his chest for a smoke.

"Yes." Gaunt shakes his head. "The poor sap."

❧

"Good morning, Mr. Clapham."

Clapham squints at Gaunt from the witness stand, nodding and murmuring a greeting. His newly clipped hair is gelled so that it stands up like wet broom straw. Gaunt takes a long pause and squints back at the witness, as though somebody else had called Clapham to testify and Gaunt couldn't imagine why. Several jurors shift restlessly in their box, and a couple of them cough. "You know," Gaunt says at last, shaking his head, "I've seen you a couple of times at the Chicken Alley, having a drink. But I almost didn't recognize you today."

Clapham chuffs through his nose and jiggles self-consciously. "Well, I'm wearing contact lenses. That could be it, I suppose."

"And your hair. It's shorter, isn't it?"

"Your Honour." Pepino rolls her eyes, as per her habitual courtroom manner. "Is this examination-in-chief or Mr. Gaunt's high school reunion?

"Save the small talk, Mr. Gaunt, for the bar — the *other* bar, I mean. The one with the chicken and the cat and the garrotter, and whatever other nasty menagerie might be in residence there." His Honour mugs for the jury.

"Actually, Your Honour," Gaunt responds. "It's quite big talk. It's sort of like, how do they say it? You can't tell the players without a program. Who's who in *The Queen against Desmond Cheshire*. Who's who at the Chicken Alley."

Looking as smug as Humpty Dumpty on his wall, the judge addresses the jury. "This case really is taking on the tone of *Malice in Wonderland*, isn't it, ladies and gentlemen? I suppose we should see where Mr. Gaunt thinks he's going with this, shouldn't we?"

"I'm obliged, Your Honour. And in fact *Alice in Wonderland* sort of comes into it, as I think Mr. Clapham will agree. You were telling us about your makeover, Mr. Clapham." Gaunt returns to the witness, smiling his slightly ghoulish, blue-toothed smile.

"Well, my girlfriend said I needed a new look. To be more with-it, I guess."

"Your girlfriend, Mr. Clapham?"

"Joy. Ms. Almundy. She gave evidence a couple of days ago."

"Ah, yes, so she did. But is she really your girlfriend? She was equivocal herself on that, I believe."

"Well, we date. We go out together."

"Mr. Clapham, I have here Exhibit Eleven, the journal of Gianna Ravenscroft. For the record, I'm putting a little yellow sticky note next to a particular line in the journal, and I'm indicating the line with an arrow on the sticky. Could you please read the line I've marked, and those following? For the jury and His Honour."

The court clerk hands the journal to the witness, who reads: "'Norm Clapham has asked me out yet again. "Normal," Joy calls him, but she doesn't know he calls her Joyless when he's with me. We have a good laugh about her, the common enemy, I guess. All's fair in love and war. For all her flaunting and flirting, Joy's actually insecure and miserable, and misery loves company, Des says, so poor Norm's her current paying guest. And does he ever pay, Des says. The cost of living isn't worth it in her case, Des says. She's always looking for attention and reassurance. Ego-stroking, Des says. Of course he calls Norm SubNormal. *Meow!* Norm is nice enough, I guess, a good friend, empathizes. I mean, he's sensitive, but he's bit of a feeb. Feckless, I think is the word. The poor wuss can't seem to accept I'm spoken for twice over. That I'm really part of the scene and he just isn't.'" The witness looks up, but Gaunt merely stares at him, until Clapham explains, blinking, only a little off kilter, "Well, yes, I asked Gianna out a couple of times. As I say, we kept each other company a lot, when our musician friends were working. But I dated Joy, too."

In the body of the courtroom Almundy looks not so much miserable as seriously browned off.

"And what's the date on that entry, Mr. Clapham, the entry in Ms. Ravenscroft's journal?"

"It seems to be January fifteenth, I guess."

"That would be two days after Mr. Wonder's death."

"Yes, I believe so."

"Did Ms. Ravenscroft ever agree to go out with you?"

"No. As you can hear in that haughty tone you get there, she was preoccupied by the pathetic delusion that she had all these celebrity suitors. The pantheon of non-wussy popular musicians. Billy says this, Des says that. I guess I tried to get her to see she was tilting at windmills. I guess I wanted to save her from herself, as a friend."

"You and Ms. Almundy both seem to have been her self-appointed therapists."

"Well, we felt sorry for her. And I liked her. So I asked her out more than once, when Joy was busy and Billy had no time for Kitten — Gianna — at all. I mean, it just seemed natural." Clapham shrugs. "We were both at a loose end. We got along well, we both had show-business connections but were outsiders, more or less. We talked about our personal lives with each other. Hopes and dreams sort of thing."

"You say she was starstruck, felt she had celebrity suitors. But before your recent makeover, be it for Ms. Almundy's or for Ms. Ravenscroft's more gothic tastes, you yourself were sort of a celebrity lookalike?"

"He's leading his witness," Pepino objects. "Or, worse, trying to put words in his mouth."

Justice Honey gives Gaunt an arch look, so that defence counsel takes a new tack. "Do you know Mr. Justice Theodore Mariner, Mr. Clapham?"

"Ted Mariner. Yes, in fact, I do. Nice guy, for a judge."

On cue, Justice Honey furrows his brow at the witness, who smiles back and continues, "Our mutual friend, I believe, Mr. Gaunt — as the title of the Dickens novel has it."

"Yet more Victorian literature, Mr. Gaunt?" With manifest distaste, Justice Honey explains to the jury that Justice Theodore Mariner is a member of this province's Court of Appeal. "Notorious, I believe, Mr. Gaunt, as a leader of that court's liberal or activist rump. Some judges like to make law, ladies and gentlemen of the jury, as though they were your elected members of Parliament. The rest of us judges think we have enough to do, thank you very much, in just interpreting the law as our elected representatives create it — as they are mandated to do by your good selves as voters. But you are to ignore anything you might have read about Justice Mariner recently in the newspapers, concerning a bit of a punch-up, I believe it was, in a restaurant. That is not in evidence, his marital difficulties and his fisticuffs or what-not. . . . With a judge, I might add, Mr. Clapham, of the Ontario Court."

"Actually, Your Honour," Gaunt says, "it didn't come to blows. It was just a little misunderstanding between colleagues."

Justice Honey nods and snuffles. "Mmm. With Mr. Justice

Cactus, I believe — a widely-respected judge of the Ontario Court of Justice who is prone to follow the law as our legislators make it. And to respect the law as a citizen trying to ease the tensions of a busy day with a quiet meal, in the company of a respectable lady friend, in a public restaurant."

Gaunt ignores the implied criticism of Justice Mariner's professionalism or lack thereof, and he asks the witness, "And what were the circumstances of your first meeting with Justice Mariner, Mr. Clapham?"

"Not in a restaurant, I hope for your health and well-being, Mr. Clapham," Justice Honey interrupts yet again.

"Your Honour," Gaunt looks heavenward, dislocating and relocating that acrobatic jaw. "I believe that Justice Mariner *and* my client are entitled to be presumed innocent."

"I don't see the relevance of this, anyway, Your Honour," Pepino objects. Presumably because she is a safer target than the judge, Gaunt takes the opportunity to vent.

"Crikey, Your Honour. If she wouldn't keep interrupting me, yet again, she'd see the relevance is that Mr. Clapham met Mr. Justice Mariner a few feet away from where Mr. Wonder was killed, and shortly before the death was discovered."

Looking genuinely interested in the answer for a change, Justice Honey asks Clapham, "You met Mr. Justice Mariner in a singles bar, Mr. Clapham? He was part of this menagerie — actually at the murder scene at the heart of this case?"

"Well, as Mr. Gaunt says, I met him at the Chicken Alley, while we were waiting for Billy Wonder and the band to play — on the night, as it happens, of Billy's death. So, in fact, it was in a restaurant, sort of. A nightclub, anyway."

"A bar!" Justice Honey harrumphs. "I imagine the Judicial Council might be interested in that, Mr. Gaunt."

"Please give us the details, Mr. Clapham," Gaunt prods the witness, studiously ignoring the presiding justice. "That's what *we're* interested in here and now. How you met . . ."

"We're all ears, in fact," Justice Honey adds.

Clapham sighs. "Well, for what it's worth, I guess he, the judge, Mr. Justice Mariner, he thought I was Des, yes. Justice Mariner came up to me and asked me for an autograph. That seems to be what Mr. Gaunt is getting at."

"Yes, Mr. Clapham," Gaunt says, breathing more easily as he turns to the jury. "It's what we call identification evidence. Who's who at the Chicken Alley. Justice Mariner thought you were Des Cheshire."

"But I mean, it was dark, for goodness' sake. I was wearing glasses and a tie and sports jacket, as Des normally does, I guess, so it was just a mistake. I'm younger, for one thing, by quite a lot. Shorter, too."

"But you were sitting down, weren't you?"

Clapham shrugs and smiles again at Justice Honey. "I mean, everyone thought it was hilarious that the judge confused me for Des. Ridiculous."

"Everyone, or just Joy?"

"It was nothing more than a silly confusion, Mr. Gaunt. As the judge soon saw, himself."

"He thought you were Des Cheshire?" Justice Honey asks, looking from the witness to the accused, who again smiles nonchalantly back at him.

"Only momentarily," Clapham answers, looking from judge to

jury. "In the dark of the nightclub. And, well, no offence to Justice Mariner, but he's not a young man any more. He wears reading glasses, you know. I think he probably needs them for more than reading, actually, but he seems a little vain about it lately. Squints around the place. Anyway, we talked about the glasses, in fact, about how he and his cat reminded me of *The Owl and the Pussycat*, from the Edward Lear poem. How his spectacles made him look owlish."

"You talked about Victorian poetry, then," Gaunt says, nodding amicably. "His Honour mentioned *Alice in Wonderland*, Mr. Clapham — after a fashion. That came up, too, didn't it, when you met Mr. Justice Mariner?" Before Pepino can object that he is leading again, Gaunt adds, "I'm only trying to help Mr. Clapham fill in the blanks for the jury, Your Honour."

"Connecting the dots, I believe is the term of legal art, Mr. Gaunt," Justice Honey says, apparently with sarcastic intent. "At least that's what I'm constantly hearing up here on the bench, whenever counsel try to sneak irrelevant evidence in."

"Well, I mean, he's admitted to speaking with Justice Mariner after the judge mistook him for my client, Des Cheshire, Your Honour." No harm in repeating that, too, for the jury. "And as far as Victorian literature goes, well the witness himself has only just brought up both Charles Dickens and Edward Lear."

"I guess he can tell us more details of their discussion, Ms. Pepino, can't he?" Justice Honey asks. "As it's already in evidence. Mind you, Mr. Gaunt, it's all taking on the irrelevant if, ahem, fascinating character of Book Television. And he'd better stick to his end of it. Otherwise" — the judge licks his lips and smiles his loose-denture grin — "you'll have to call Mr. Justice Mariner to testify." Justice Honey somehow resists rubbing his hands.

"Well, I teach at Ryerson University, you see," Clapham continues, "and Victorian social history is my specialty. So Justice Mariner and I, well, we talked about literature of that period, the Victorian period. As a social historian, I'm interested in those little quirky social artifacts, like the nonsense poetry. It fleshes out the dustier facts, gets some blood coursing through history's veins, although my students don't seem to feel it much. They'd rather be playing computer games or drinking beer, I guess. But Justice Mariner gets it. He's quite well read, as you know. Although he tends to prefer the sixteenth century . . ."

"So you're an expert on Victorian social history?" Gaunt wrestles the witness back on point and safe from the pitfalls of hearsay. "The blood and guts of the time, as you were suggesting."

Clapham suddenly goes modest. "Well, I haven't finished my thesis yet, Mr. Gaunt. I've been a little slow about it. That's why I'm only a sessional teacher at, well, you know, at a sort of second-tier school, a vocational college on steroids, really — Ry High, the students call it, where, by the way, I don't get to teach my specialty at all, in fact. Because I'm not a full Ph.D., you see. I'm stuck, I'm afraid, with Introduction to Canadian History, which is a required course that nobody wants to teach or take, especially at eight o'clock in the morning."

"That sounds rather frustrating," Gaunt commiserates.

"Yes. And on top of it, I have to teach a remedial research and writing course. For students who somehow got into the 'university'" — Clapham uses his fingers to add quotation marks for the court — "without literacy skills."

"Not really making the best use of your training and talent."

"Well, no, they're not. It's frustrating, as you say. Very. But I'm hoping to have my thesis all wrapped up this time next year, and to get on with my career." Clapham fails miserably at looking optimistic.

"Hoping. And how long have you been working on your doctoral degree, then? A while, I take it, from what Justice Mariner has told me." Gaunt shoots a what-are-you-going-to-do-about-it look at Justice Honey.

"Well, I've had to get two extensions, unfortunately. It's almost twelve years, I'm embarrassed to say. I've had some trouble with depression, you see." Clapham glances up at Justice Honey, who is tracing circles on his desk again. "It tends to paralyze you, just about. I mean, when it really hits. Clinical depression. Creates this inertia that's like the weight of the world. And then they put you on pills that can have side effects, like make you light-headed or sick at your stomach, or interfere with your concentration, or even with your ability to reason as well you would like. I'm borderline bipolar, apparently, swinging between depression and euphoria, you see. So, well, to make a long story short, I'm still working on my expert status, Mr. Gaunt. But I'm nearly there."

"Nearly there. And you're how old now, Mr. Clapham?"

"Well, I'll be thirty-six this month."

"Middle age on the horizon, then, eh?"

"That's pushing it a bit, isn't Mr. Gaunt?" Justice Honey grumbles.

"Perhaps, Your Honour, perhaps. But still frustrating, frustrating, frustrating, eh Mr. Clapham? Poor Norm, as Ms. Ravenscroft put it. The two of you in therapy, frustrated, sad, commiserating. Holding hands." Gaunt puts on his I-just-hate-to-suggest-this voice: "Subnormal."

The witness smiles sadly.

"Twelve years," Gaunt continues, "and struggling along at a second-tier school, not really in your field, fighting depression and anxiety, getting on in life with no committed girlfriend, the girls calling you a wussy. Poor old Norman. . . ."

Pepino steps on Gaunt's manifest, um, empathy. "First of all, Your Honour, he's leading like it's his high school reunion again and he's invited Mr. Clapham to dance his clinical depression away. Second, if Mr. Gaunt wants to continue in this vein, he's going to have to qualify Mr. Clapham as an expert, and I have to tell him that I'm going to take Mr. Clapham's own position, that he's no expert. I mean, what the heck are we talking about Victorian social history for, anyway? It's all very educational, but it's also confusing for the jury, and the rest of us, I dare say."

"Yes, Mr. Gaunt," the judge snuffles. "It's time for Alice and the pussycat to move back above ground, into the real world, in real time."

"Mr. Clapham," Gaunt persists, "to cut to the chase, speaking simply as a student of social history and no expert, would you study not just the poetry but the everyday life of those Victorian times, which I take to be the early-to-mid-eighteen hundreds to the end of the century?"

"Exactly, Mr. Gaunt. As I mentioned, that's what a social historian does." Gaunt has engaged Clapham's pedantic, and relieved, interest in himself and his subject. "He or she studies the history of the times through the everyday life. The blood and guts, as you aptly put it."

"Including, say, what people of the day read?"

"We've been over that, Mr. Gaunt." Justice Honey's voice has risen several decibels. "Let's not revisit it, lest you put us all to sleep. Yes?"

"What they ate and drank?" Gaunt continues. "The popular music? Their sex lives?"

"Sometimes, yes."

"The crimes they committed?"

"Absolutely."

"Absolutely. The blood and guts. And as a student of Victorian crime, Mr. Clapham, please tell the jury what you have learned about the year 1862. Anything bloody and gutsy stand out about that date?"

"Eighteen sixty-two, Mr. Gaunt?"

"Yes, anything unusual about criminal activity in Victorian England around then? From the viewpoint of a student of social history?"

"Oh, yes. I see what you mean. There was a notorious rash of street robberies. Yes, now that you mention it. In London. Eighteen sixty-two into 1863. It caused quite a ruckus about law and order, a real hub-bub among the chattering classes."

"And what made the robberies distinctive? I mean, why was there such a ruckus?"

"Well, because there were a lot of the same kind of them," Clapham temporizes. "All concentrated in the same area. Street robberies."

Gaunt is unfazed. "Same kind, how, Mr. Clapham?"

"Well, the robbers all throttled their victims with, you know, wire or whatever. With rope, I guess. You know, they used, they strangled, or, you know . . ."

"Is the word you're searching for 'garrotted,' Mr. Clapham?

Garrotting was so rife in the streets, the government decided that the robbers would be assiduously flogged for it?"

Pepino leaps to her feet and shouts, "He's leading like Fred Astaire with Ginger Rogers, for cripe's sake!"

"I don't see the harm, Ms. Pepino," the judge says mildly, leaning on one hand while admiring the doodling finger of the other, obviously more interested in the evidence now than in the niceties of criminal procedure. He looks up. "Personally, I've always thought it would be salubrious to bring back the cat. It used to be in our own *Criminal Code*, you know, members of the jury. Whipping for certain serious crimes. As late as 1972. With the good ol' cat o' nine tails."

"Yes, sir," Mortimer agrees, rising to assist the court in its fond reminiscences. "When I first entered practice, the *Code* sanctioned whipping for sexual offences and robbery. I believe it was a possible penalty for possessing marijuana, too, up to 1955." I can't be sure, but I think I hear Pepino mutter *The good old days* under her breath, throwing her co-counsel a skeptical look. She has, after all, several admirable qualities, which no doubt you will have noticed.

The judge smiles nostalgically, nodding and warming to the witness. "And there was a mandatory seven-year prison sentence, besides. But the whipping. You know, I always thought it was a shame we didn't actually use such provisions more often. I mean, as an example to all criminals. General deterrence. They act like naughty children, treat them as such. It works terrifically well in Singapore. Public caning, I mean." Justice Honey shakes his head wistfully. "It's a very clean and orderly country, you know, Singapore, Mr. Clapham."

"The mere threat of it worked a treat in this instance, too, Your

Honour," Gaunt fauns, keen to recover his advantage. "Stopped the garrotting problem on a dime. Or a shilling, I guess."

"Actually, that's a myth, Your Honour." Joining in the general clamour to gain favour with the irascible court, Clapham stomps all over Gaunt's scholarship. "In 1938, the British government looked into corporal punishment in the sentencing of criminals. They have a long history there of flogging prisoners, and using it in their schools, too. They found that Queen Victoria's whipping threat didn't deter a thing." He smirks at Gaunt. "Speaking ABD — as a student, but not quite a qualified expert."

"ABD, Mr. Clapham?" the judge asks, smiling vaguely.

"All but dissertation, Your Honour. Thesis." Given — or more likely because of — the judge's sympathetic reception of his evidence, Clapham has gone quite red, and his hands are balled up in fists only slighter larger than Joy Almundy's. "I mean, I'm not quite as feckless and feeble as Mr. Gaunt would have you believe."

Gaunt turns briefly to Nadia Hussein with a look that would be black if it weren't enlivened with sadistic pleasure, a look that jubilantly hollers *Who's so smart, now?* at her. Unfortunately, she has left the courtroom. In compensation, or to further prove himself an advocate one should never underestimate, Gaunt employs Clapham's pedantic correction to his full advantage. "We'll get back to how feckless you might or might not be, Normal, er, Mr. Clapham. But clearly it was a notorious crime of the day, this garrotting business, and it is still discussed among students of Victorian social history?"

"Yes, yes," Clapham agrees, but with an air of growing fury. "Yes, Mr. Gaunt, it was a very interesting little epidemic, for us students."

"Indeed," Gaunt agrees, smiling while Justice Honey suddenly scowls, not at all pleased to discover that whipping is effective only among sexual fetishists.

"And so as to avoid my leading you into anything, Mr. Clapham" — Gaunt nods at opposing counsel — "could you now simply read the next line in Ms. Ravenscroft's journal? The line following the passage you read earlier, about how you asked her out and she was spoken for?"

"Where do you mean? She says I asked her out, and she was spoken for, and I'm not good enough for her or whatever. Poor, feckless me, right, Mr. Gaunt? Blah blah. Then there's just a bunch of signatures. Is that what you mean? Like an idiot school-girl would write. 'Gianna Cheshire,' it looks like. 'Mrs. Gianna Ravenscroft-Cheshire.' 'Gianna and Des Cheshire,' I think. And *I'm* the feckless one."

"This upsets you, doesn't it Mr. Clapham?"

"Leading, Mr. Gaunt," Justice Honey says.

"Well, tell us, Mr. Clapham, in your own words, how does that make you feel? How *did* that make you feel, that Gianna seems to have had feelings for Mr. Cheshire, even though he'd warned her off Billy Wonder and Billy Wonder was now gone, and there you are waiting patiently in the wings, caring and sensitive old Norman, willing and available to take Billy's place? Her confessor and confidant?"

"I don't know what you're getting at, Mr. Gaunt. I can only tell you that she told me herself how Billy was hers forever, and that they had a lovers' pact to die together if the world wouldn't recognize their undying love. She said it was encoded in his music. A lovers' pact. She was into death, Kitten was, the black arts and all that, the whole Goth thing, and she used to say how poets called sex the little death. So to her mind sex and death were linked."

"Erotomania, I believe that's called."

"Counsel's giving evidence," Pepino objects. "He's using his own witness as a straw man."

But Clapham is not to be interrupted. "And she said Billy was sending her these love and death messages in his music. So her sudden interest in Des seemed just more of this casting about — some sort of shock reaction or whatever to Billy's death. That's all. Some sort of coping thing, maybe at the enormity of what she'd done. Possibly. I mean, I'm not necessarily saying she killed Billy. Or even that Des killed Billy. Or even that they did it together. I don't know, Mr. Gaunt. I know she was a very troubled person. And I'm not surprised to hear that she's killed herself. But as you say, I'm not an expert at anything in particular. I'm just poor, feckless Normal."

"That's fascinating, Mr. Clapham. Gianna's a sort of Goth or Satanist. She's called you pathetic and feckless. She might have killed Billy. She might be suicidal. She rejects your advances. Then, before his corpse is cold, she professes an interest in Des Cheshire, and you're still interested in dating her?"

"Well, a lot of that stuff she did was just for show. Actually she was shy, Mr. Gaunt, a lovely, caring person. Attractive under all that make-up, smart, creative, sexy. Justice Mariner said that, himself. She was a lost soul. Confused. Casting about."

"He can't tell us what Mr. Justice Mariner said," Pepino objects.

"You might want to call him as a witness, Mr. Gaunt," Justice Honey suggests.

"She just needed help," Clapham continues. "Someone who

cared. She was troubled and lonely and vulnerable, sort of little-girlish, really, and I thought I could change that."

"Exploit it or change it?" Gaunt asks. "Compared to Joy Almundy, she was easy pickings, wasn't she, Mr. Clapham? A lonely little girl, for a lonely, depressed guy? A Muse you thought you could actually conquer? A tower you could climb? Only you couldn't, could you, any more than she could conquer Billy or Des?"

"Your Honour," Melody Pepino wearily objects again, "he's cross-examining his own witness."

"I'm sorry, Your Honour," Gaunt replies. "I was just trying to connect the dots. For the jury." Gaunt smiles bleakly at those twelve fact-finders good and true. Fortuitously, Nadia Hussein comes through the doors at the back of the room, bows hurriedly to the bench, and sprints up to Gaunt to whisper in his ear.

"We're waiting, counsel," Justice Honey says. "I think we've kept this witness long enough as it is."

Poker-faced, Gaunt turns back to Norman Clapham. "I'm sorry, Your Honour. Mr. Clapham, what if I said this to you: 'Keep cool, but don't freeze?' That mean anything to you?"

"Mean anything?" Clapham has gone rigid and white — frozen, you might say — but he giggles. "No, nothing in partic-ular. It's certainly not Victorian verse. Sounds like what your doctor would tell you about how to survive the winter here."

"You sure about that?"

"Quite."

"Wasn't that perhaps the contents of a note given to you by Gianna Ravenscroft?"

"It could have been. She gave me various writings out of her notebook. Poems. Half-baked songs. Stuff like that. None of it particularly memorable. Most of it doggerel or mystical, childish tripe. Pathetic, self-involved nonsense. Generally I just threw it away."

"Really? But this particular message was by way of a Dear John letter, wasn't it? Or, in this case, a Dear Normal letter? Quite memorable, indeed. So memorable that you carried it around in your pocket?"

"I don't know what you're talking about, Mr. Gaunt."

"What if I told you that the police have just discovered your fingerprints on a supposed suicide note, along with what they think is a bit of the old Harris tweed, from a dress jacket, perhaps? And that they found the note itself near Ms. Ravenscroft, as she lay on her bed, strangled to death in the same way Billy Wonder was strangled? A note that said, 'Keep cool but don't freeze'? A note torn from her diary. A note, I don't know, a note that maybe you chucked back in her face — threw away, indeed — after she gave it to you to let you down gently, a note trying to inform you in a nice way that she wasn't really interested in you romantically, gently saying you can't really conquer your Muse. A note that you left in her room, perhaps, as a statement, a note of sarcasm, call it . . . after you strangled her to death, just like you strangled Billy Wonder?"

CHAPTER 17

The Best Is Yet to Come

"It's just poking around at this stage." Izzy Finster was at pains to reassure the Mariners as they sat across from him in his office in Law Chambers that morning, eleven floors above University Avenue. The window facing the couple framed the illuminated weather beacon on the Canada Life Building, and the beacon had gone red, for stormy weather. I was locked down in the judge's chambers, of course, on my Humpty Dumpty cot, under the divan, camouflaged by a sofa shawl . . . banged up in quarters that resembled a prison cell all the more when you considered that my toilet facilities were just two sofa legs away. But needs must: we didn't want to get nobbled by the Government Services cleaners. And so I have had to reconstruct what follows from discussions in said chambers later the same week.

"Somebody has complained about you, Ted, to the Judicial Council," Finster seems to have said. "Normally, the chair or vice-chair would screen the complaint, maybe talk to the Chief Justice about your boyish shenanigans." Finster grinned at Penny, at least in my mind's eye.

"Yes, thanks, Izzy," Justice Mariner said. "Highly amusing."

"But if the complainant was somebody like Cactus, a judge of the Ontario Court, well, it pretty well had to be passed along to the Conduct Committee, screening or not. That's what this will be about."

"But I talked to Hernando myself, " Mrs. Mariner said.

"Again," Justice Mariner observed. "Charming."

"He seemed to think it was all best forgotten."

"Don't we all?" Justice Mariner added, staring at his lap, no doubt.

"I'm sure your intervention was seriously considered, Penny. But, well, once the thing's set in motion, you know," Finster explained, "they still have to ask a few questions, even if just for appearance's sake. So they've appointed Tristan Chase as independent counsel, to see if there's anything to it."

"I don't get it, Izzy. If Cactus is over it, why aren't they?" Justice Mariner asked. "Unless." He raised an index finger, his eyes roving upward to survey the dark clouds of his imaginings. "Unless! Yep. I bet it's not Cactus at all, Pen. I bet you it's that old grumblebelly, Justice Honey, sticking his oar in, brought down specially from his beloved cottage on Georgian Bay, just to stir things up. Because of the evidence at the Cheshire trial. Lee Gaunt says Honey's been licking his lips about me being at the murder scene."

"We'll have to see." Finster shrugged. "Anyway, my advice is the same you would give your own clients. Keep your answers short and to the point. Don't give them any more rope to hang — or garrotte — you with."

"Lovely. Hanging judges hanging judges."

Penny put her hand on her husband's. "Don't be ridiculous, Ted. You heard Izzy. It's a formality." Husband and wife exchanged sad smiles. But it was not that simple. . . .

⚬ჿ⚬

"Mr. Justice Cactus has very generously decided to withdraw his complaint," Tristan Chase says after the social niceties are transacted. Justice Mariner exchanges terse smiles again with his wife, who sits once more to his left, with Izzy Finster at right flank, now in Chase's office on the forty-ninth floor of the Toronto-Dominion Tower. They face Chase's certificate from the Law Society stating that he is a specialist in civil litigation. In fact, the independent counsel's usual specialty is defending doctors accused of diddling their patients in one way or another, negligently or with lascivious intent. And Chase looks every bit the middle-level partner in the litigation department of a high-flyer Bay Street firm, in this case, Huffernan Sylvester: Slender, angular, blue-eyed is he, and literally the golden-haired boy, never mind that he's in his early forties.

"I'm not sure it's all that generous, Tris, in the circumstances," Finster says. "It takes two to tango."

Unfortunately, this emboldens Justice Mariner to add bitterly, "Ol' Prickly wasn't exactly a model of judicial comportment himself. And he probably snitched me out just because the better man won — because Penny and I are reconciling, Tris."

But then there is Justice Honey and his oar. Finster squeezes Justice Mariner's arm as Chase continues, raising his voice at first, "Be that as it may, Judge, we are advised that you currently live" — Chase checks his notes — "upstairs in a condemned bar" — Chase takes a beat to peer at Justice Mariner over his reading glasses, and Justice Mariner returns the favour, as though it's the Showdown at the Bifocal Corral — "you live over a bar in the company of an ageing tomcat with violent propensities." Chase sits back and removes his eyeglasses, dropping his papers on his desk. "And that you spend most afternoons, and every night, in the bar proper."

"Violent propensities? Ageing?" The judge looks grimly at the ceiling, sighing and leaning back in his chair. "More of a lover than a fighter, I'd say."

"Ted," Penny says. "It's not about the cat."

"Who says I'm talking about the cat?" Justice Mariner turns to Tristan Chase. "And, by the bye, Chase, the Alley's not 'condemned.' Just a little tired, like the rest of us ageing geezers, here. Undergoing repairs."

"The thing is, though, Ted," Chase says, "it really is kind of a two-peas-in-a-pod situation, isn't it? People can't seem to tell if, in fact, *you're* an ageing lover or an ageing fighter, eh?"

"People?" Mrs. Mariner says, out of the judge's side of her mouth, and so that only her husband can hear. "His own family could use help on figuring that one out."

The judge glances sideways at his wife before addressing the younger lion. "Look, Tris. As you've just said yourself, Hernando's decided that the unfortunate contretemps in Pasta La Vista was something and nothing. I mean, we've all agreed, I think, that it was just a misunderstanding all around, and that it was out of character for everyone."

Both Penny and Finster purse their lips, like constipated bookends. Finally, Penny says, "Let's just not go there, Ted. Not again."

"No, let's not," Chase agrees. "I think all we'll get is indigestion."

Finster and Chase find this highly risible.

"Anyway, the bar proper, as you put it," Justice Mariner says, "happens to be where my old friend Jersey Doucette spends his days working, earning his meagre crust. We go way back, Jersey and I, and I've just been helping out in the bar — only in the last little while, I might add — pitching in as a friend, chatting with him and giving him a hand down there. That's it. The only thing that passes my lips is the occasional soft drink. Cranberry juice, orange juice. Jersey's saved my bacon more than once over the years, Tris. I put myself through law school working for him at the Chicken Alley. He's been very good to me, and I won't have him, or his completely legitimate business, slagged off like this." His Lordship crosses his arms. "You might say that Jersey Doucette's made me the man I am today."

"Yes, I suppose you might," Chase grimly agrees.

"I'm not ashamed of either one of us."

"I'm not saying you should be, Ted. Don't get me wrong. But you have to consider the appearance of the thing, to Joe and Jane Citizen. I'm sure you're generally as sober as a judge." When no one on the defence side cracks a smile, Chase continues. "But the public doesn't know that, do they? They see you hanging around a bar at all hours. They're bound to wonder, is this guy bringing his full faculties to his job? *Is* he sober as a judge? And even the toniest saloons attract the dissolute, the criminal element, the, excuse me, Mrs. Mariner, the loose ladies."

"I think I can handle the terminology describing my husband's associates, Mr. Chase," Penny Mariner advises. "It's what they might be getting up to that I'm concerned about." She casts an ironic regard at His Lordship. *I see my wife in spirit. Her regard, / Like yours, amiable creature, / Profound and cold, cuts and splits like snake tongues dart . . .*

"Well, exactly. And Mr. Doucette's customers are just as likely to be before you at the capital-b Bar, Ted, as next to you at that small-b bar, this Alley place. How can the public be sure you're deciding the cases fairly when you might be rubbing elbows and toasting good health with criminal appellants, or their friends and family, or standing drinks for guys cheating on the wives who are divorcing them?"

"How, indeed?" Mrs. Mariner mutters again for her spouse's private benefit.

"You can't really say I'm overstating the case, can you, Ted? I mean, look — there was a murder in this place, and you were seated only a few feet away from it, I'm told." Chase returns his spectacles to his face, mostly, it seems, so that he can peer over them judicially at the judge, reversing the usual roles of the court-room drama.

"Look, Tris. As you've probably heard, yes, Penny and I have had a few problems lately. Which really are the origin of everything that's brought us here. But we've worked all that out now. In the interim, Jersey was good enough to take me and the little cat in. As a friend. A good, old friend. That's the whole Chicken Alley story, beginning to end. And as you can see, Penny's here to support me this morning. Plus, I'm happy to say we've agreed that I'll be moving back home this very day. As soon as we're done here. We've reconciled completely. I won't be staying in the condemned bar, as you put it, or consorting regularly with poor old raggedy-arsed Jersey."

"Well, I'm sure the Judicial Conduct Committee will be pleased to hear it."

"So it's all settled, then."

"Well, no, Ted, unfortunately not — not by a long shot. There is still the matter of your articled clerk."

"Sorry?"

"The student. We understand that there might have been some inappropriate touching."

Penny Mariner removes her hand from that of her allegedly reconciled spouse.

"The student herself is not complaining. But we can't be too careful these days with that sort of thing. Particularly where there are some cross-cultural considerations. And you'll appreciate, I hope, that there's a considerable power imbalance — appeal justice, law student. You have to be like Caesar's wife, you know, or Desdemona, anyhow, above reproach. Times have changed, Ted."

As Justice Mariner sits open-mouthed, and manifestly not powerful at all, fortunately he has counsel present to assist him. "Tris," Finster says, "we had no notice of any such complaint. Times changing or not. And if the student isn't complaining. . . ."

"Would you please stop calling her 'the student'?" Justice Mariner cries. In mid-level dudgeon, he glances from Chase, to Penny, to Finster. "This girl's a firecracker, Tris. She can take care of herself. She's bright, one of the best clerks I've ever had. And she's no pushover, let alone a shrinking violet. She's as assertive as they come. Which, combined with her intelligence, makes her very good at what she does. And not afraid to pipe up if it's appropriate. Personally, I can't believe she's complained of me."

"As I've said in the past, you certainly seem to have gotten to know her," Penny adds, not entirely helpfully, as she crosses her arms and looks at Chase, her new ally in the war between the sexes. "Very well. Personally."

"Penny, she's my *student*."

"I thought you said we were to call her the Firecracker."

Chase steps in as referee. "As I say, you both should know that the student — Ms. Hussein — did not herself complain. Word has got back to us from one of the other students. I take it they simply discussed it, as colleagues."

"Personally, I don't find that reassuring," Penny says, glaring at her husband.

"We approached the student, however," Chase goes on, "Ms. Hussein, that is, as part of our investigation. And she has asked to attend this morning, to make a statement."

"A statement? What kind of statement?" Finster intervenes, lurching forward in his seat.

"I think you should just hear her out."

Finster glances at Justice Mariner, who rolls his eyes, flops back in his chair and says "God in Heaven," although I have not previously known him to appeal to any higher authority beyond the Norton anthologies of literature. Finster tells Chase: "We'll hear her out, Tris, but I want it on the record that we had no notice of any complaint of this nature, and we're reserving our right to object to any further action on or use of what transpires here today."

Now it's Chase's turn to purse his lips. "Just hear her out, please, Mr. Finster." He brings Nadia Hussein into the room and, bold as brass (or as bold as Baudelaire rising fortuitously from the dead at my own lynching), she shakes hands with Mrs. Mariner and Isadore Finster, then nods to Justice Mariner while saying, "Your Honour."

Chase invites Hussein to sit at the corner of his desk, and taking the seat she says, "Your Honour, I am here to state up front that I did not appreciate at all that you kissed me in the Chicken Alley while we were working on the Des Cheshire file."

"You kissed her?" Penny wants to know, from the accused himself.

"I don't think so," the judge says mildly, and it's clear he's sincere. "I mean, if I did, it was not a moving violation."

"Well, that's just it," Hussein continues, unfazed. "I was very offended, at first, but then I realized that you didn't mean anything by it at all."

"I didn't?" the judge asks.

"He didn't?" Penny Mariner asks, her eyes still locked like Taser guns on her husband.

"It was reflexive, I believe. You were just carried away by the moment. And perhaps male menopause, I am told. Mental incapacity, as our law calls it. Guilty but not responsible. Non-insane automatism. A sort of mid-life virus."

"That's certainly possible, Nadia," the judge confesses, nodding at his student and smiling sadly. "There seems to be a lot of it going around. And my life has been like that lately." He turns to his wife. "Emotional. Confused. Lonely. Working stuff out. That I can admit."

"But we're not formally admitting it," Finster hastily adds.

"Personally, I'm taking it as a full confession," Mrs. Mariner says.

"Please, Mrs. Mariner, if you'll let me finish." Hussein turns back to the accused, standing to address him and the jury. "You've been going through a very stressful time, estranged from your lady wife, living miserably over that horrible old saloon with all those junkies and musicians and prostitutes."

"Consorting with all sorts," Penny harrumphs, looking student Hussein up and down.

"It's in Yorkville!" His Lordship spreads his hands, speaking pleadingly to Tris Chase. "One of the poshest neighbourhoods in town. And it's not condemned!"

"Searching for answers from pop psychologists on the afternoon television programs," Hussein continues.

"Terminal male menopause," Penny says.

"I hadn't realized we'd reached the punishment phase already," the judge says. "Public humiliation. The bloody pillory."

"In that regard, I assure you we've only just begun," Penny Mariner assures him. "Your Honour."

"But really, Mrs. Mariner, from working with your husband I know him to be a fine, truly honourable man." Hussein smiles glowingly at Penny and begins pacing at the side of Chase's desk, which rather obviously seems to make the golden boy nervous. "With a capital h for Your Honour. A role model. One of the few people I have met in my career at the bar, short though it is, who truly understands the distinction between law and justice. A mentor who is truly more interested in the latter."

His Lordship sits back in his chair, grinning at his student while looking like he could just as easily weep. "And so," Hussein concludes her closing argument for the defence, "I thought that, if Your Honour was going to be my role model, I should do justice, as well, and temper it with mercy. And common sense."

"Just like fair Portia of Venice." Justice Mariner nods.

"Just like Portia, citing to *The Merchant of Venice* by William Shakespeare, year sixteen zero zero." Nadia Hussein smiles. "'To do a great right,' Portia advises, 'do a little wrong.'" Inevitably, the Bard has stuck *his* oar in again.

"Actually," Justice Mariner says, raising a long but slightly arthritic finger once more. "Bassanio says that. And, really, Portia rejects it. Everybody thinks she says bend the law, but in fact, she's all for enforcing the black letter of the law. You can have your pound of flesh, she insists, but there's nothing that says you can spill any blood getting it. She's a real lawyer's lawyer. Make your cut but draw no blood. One pound exactly, and not even a fraction of an ounce more."

"Shut up, Ted," Penny hisses in the judge's ear. "Before you lose several pounds of flesh. You're just digging another hole for yourself with your French-kissing tongue."

"In any event," Nadia Hussein concludes, "I just want to tell these good people that His Honour is not only an amateur Shakespearean scholar, but a fine, very professional jurist, and that he gives offence only to provide the best defence. Only, that is, because he cares about justice more than about the black letter of the law. He is most certainly *not* a lawyer's lawyer."

"Thank you," the judge says. "I think."

Carried away with her own compassion and eloquence, Hussein is not finished. "He hugs and kisses, lady and gentlemen, only to celebrate the victory of justice in a system where you are presumed innocent until a fair trial decides otherwise. And I can't imagine how the Judicial Council — or you, Mrs. Justice Mariner, as chief judicial officer in the Mariner matrimonial home — I can't imagine how you could possibly object to that."

"That's my student," Justice Mariner says, beaming. "A reasonable doubt, at a reasonable price."

CHAPTER 18

Tea for Two

Upon hearing of Gianna Ravenscroft's violent demise, Lawrence Hafner, M.D., has agreed to testify via satellite teleconferencing as the last witness in *Her Majesty the Queen versus Eugene Desmond Cheshire*. Even on TV, and in that often arid limbo of middle age that seems to have caused an epidemic of panic around me, Hafner is rather handsome (by Has-being reckoning), with fine features, a full head of dark, wavy hair, and a ready smile. He is nothing like the lugubrious, Teutonic stereotype humans favour for their psychiatrists. Gaunt elicits from the suave soul doctor that, with the rise of the modern cult of celebrity ("the *People* magazine syndrome," Hafner calls it), the diagnosis of erotomania has become much more common. "Typically," he explains, "the patient suffers from the delusion that a famous or powerful person — a movie star, a rock singer, your prime minister — is infatuated with her. In Ms. Ravenscroft's case, I believe the musician Billy Wonder was primarily the love-object. Typically again, the erotomaniac obsessively attempts to contact the celebrity, sometimes stalking the person and eventually, in a frenzy of frustrated intention, conquering him, in the patient's mind, by doing violence to the love-object. There can be a lot of jealousy involved, a really potent stew of erotic and violent emotions. It can be very dangerous."

"What if others intervene to try to stop the harassment?" Gaunt asks.

"Often, this only strengthens the delusion, even if we lock the patient away in the hospital or a prison to protect herself as well as the object of her unwanted attentions." Hafner lists prominent victims of erotomaniacs: TV talk-show host David Letterman, musician George Harrison (whose stalker stabbed him), the British newscaster Jill Dando (killed by her stalker), writer Germaine Greer, film director Steven Spielberg, the movie star Meg Ryan. . . .

"The syndrome was identified in the nineteen-twenties by the French psychiatrist Gaëtan de Clérambault," Hafner explains. "He had a middle-aged patient who insisted that the king of England, George V, was in love with her. She haunted Buckingham Palace, interpreting even the twitching of the window curtains as *billets doux* to her from His Majesty — signals of his amorous interest in her.

"Clérambault identified three stages of the syndrome: hope, defiance, and hatred. When the patient's hopes about the supposed love affair are constantly spurned, she gets defiant and insistent that it exists anyway. When she's further frustrated in her pursuit, she can grow to hate the love-object, and sometimes those who are close to that person, particularly if the erotomaniac sees them as barriers between herself and the love-object. Other times the delusional person will use violence to impress the love-object. Some observers claim that John Hinckley is an example of this. They say he shot President Ronald Reagan to impress the movie star Jodie Foster."

"And when I asked you about this syndrome over the phone yesterday," Gaunt says, "we were talking about how it could sort of be infectious."

"Well, you can't exactly catch it from someone else. What we were discussing, Mr. Gaunt, is a distinct psychiatric phenomenon, often called *folie à deux*, a sort of mutual delusion. It's related to erotomania in the sense that both are forms of paranoia, in medical terms. The *folie* usually involves two people who are very close, one dominant, the other more submissive. They have this very exciting, mutually affirming relationship based on a feeling of mutual persecution, usually. But often it diminishes or vanishes when the two people separate. It's a matter of 'I can't be crazy if somebody else agrees with me.' Particularly for the submissive person."

In cross-examination, Melody Pepino establishes that Dr. Hafner had never known Gianna Ravenscroft as violent. In fact, he accepts Pepino's description that, "mostly she acted like a dozey, somewhat troubled adolescent, not like a crazy person." Pepino then has the psychiatrist confirm that he had never met, let alone examined, any of Ravenscroft's friends or acquaintances — particularly not Norman Clapham — and that the chances of Ravenscroft's participating in any sort of shared delusion with "someone such as Mr. Clapham is highly speculative at best."

This will not stop Leland Gaunt from putting the proposition to the jury, anyway — as raising a reasonable doubt that his client, Eugene Desmond Cheshire, had murdered his longtime musical partner, the late, great Billy Wonder.

PART THREE

Finale:
Seems Like Old Times

(Allegro con sentimento)

CHAPTER 19

Seems Like Old Times

"I guess I gotta be throwin' him some kinda damn party or some such now, don't I?" Jersey grumbled. The question was rhetorical, of course, given that the old coot had already ordered special party food and extra champagne, which the Liquor Control Board of Ontario provided with "free occasion-appropriate stemware," as long as you forked over the breakage deposit. And Jersey had dragooned Nadia Hussein and Leland Gaunt into kitchen duty. When last I had seen them they were in the bar proper, where they had exhausted an entire roll of the kitchen's parchment paper, under injunction issued by Jersey to make a banner that said

THEY THOUGHT HE WAS A GONER BUT
THE CHESHIRE CAT CAME BACK!!!
GET OUT OF JAIL FREE, DES!!!

For the first time in known history, the current and former law clerks operated in full collaboration, trading wisecracks and even agreeing to attend Des's coming-out party as each other's "occasion-appropriate date." I wouldn't go so far as to call it mating season, but . . .

⟋⟍

Of course, when the police discovered Gianna Ravenscroft dead at the sorority house cum bed-and-breakfast on Madison Avenue, Justice Mariner and Leland Gaunt were obliged to revise their defence strategy in *The Queen v. Cheshire.* Their original idea had been to raise a reasonable doubt by suggesting that Ravenscroft, or perhaps Joy Almundy, was more likely to have killed Billy Wonder. A woman scorned and all that. Naturally, having originally structured his case that way, Gaunt alluded to the two women in his closing address to the jury. Then, too, he was careful to note that the angry and frequently strung-out comic, Tommy Profitt, had disappeared immediately after the Wonder murder, absconding in the middle of his gig at the Chicken Alley following a history of rocky relations with Billy as his employer. But there was no denying that, in all the circumstances (as we like to say over at the Court of Appeal), the most incriminating evidence pointed to Norman Clapham — "a man with a history of clinical depression," Gaunt pointed out to the jury, "frustrated at every turn, in his professional life, his everyday private life, and particularly in his romantic life.

"In that context, imagine Mr. Clapham's feelings about Billy Wonder, a rival for the affections of Ms. Ravenscroft, but also as Ms. Ravenscroft's friend and brother-confessor concerning Mr. Wonder. Imagine how, relegated to being 'just friends,' Mr. Clapham must have felt justified in his anger at Billy Wonder by the fact that Ms. Ravenscroft was murderously angry at the bandleader herself, for what *she* felt in her turn as ardent love spurned. As Dr. Hafner has explained, she would have been in that third, dangerous phase of erotomania, the so-called hatred phase. And there was Mr. Clapham, the submissive suitor, fully capable of identifying with her state of mind. Imagine, members of the jury, how this sad old 'Normal' must have seen the opportunity to play at being the exciting and romantic white knight, coming to the rescue of his fair maiden — or gothic anti-fair maiden — in their mutual delusion, this *folie à deux*, as Dr. Hafner has explained it. This delusion for two, this deadly game of chess in which he slayed Billy the Black Knight of Wonderland.

"And consider this, members of the jury: What, really, would Mr. Clapham risk in killing Billy Wonder in such a dramatic fashion? Everyone knew of Des Cheshire's troubled relationship with Mr. Wonder. The one-sided contract, the royalties, the differing visions about repertoire. . . . If any harm came to Billy, Des would immediately be the prime suspect. And how convenient to dispose of two rivals — supposed rivals, anyway, for Ms. Ravenscroft, of course — with one move . . . or garrotte. Then, too, Wonder's world was one of bars and nightclubs, Hollywood and Harlem, not to mention after-hours Yorkville with its high-end crack addicts and supermodel escorts. It was an alleycat world, full of professional and sexual jealousy, bar-hopping, bed-hopping (as His Honour put it), guns, knives, tempers, and mind-altering substances. Darkness, ladies and gentlemen, and all the creatures of the night. And of course celebrities like Billy Wonder were always at risk from the over-ardent fan, unfortunates such as Ms. Ravenscroft. So, obviously, any number of people could have made up the police list of suspects in the Wonder murder. Including Ms. Ravenscroft." Gaunt clicked the old jaw. "Including Ms. Almundy."

Click the other direction. "Including other musicians, or even John or Jane Doe off the street." *Click.* "And especially including Mr. Norman Clapham.

"Yes, given that he cared so much for Gianna, at one time, anyway, you might expect that Mr. Clapham would have wanted to spare her being investigated by the police. But consider what he had to lose, even if ultimately the police pinned the crime on her. Mr. Clapham knew that Ms. Ravenscroft was mentally unstable. We're talking about an educated man, here, members of the jury, a man who knew all about garrotting, for example, and mid-Victorian England. He would also have known that, if Gianna Ravenscroft were convicted of the murder, she could well have avoided prison. Probably she simply would have been hospitalized for a few years, and she needed the help in any event. What was the harm? She would have been, as the law puts it, guilty but not criminally responsible — conducted to the hospital, to be treated, in that quaint old phrase, 'at Her Majesty's pleasure.' A ward of the compassionate state.

"But then, much of the time Ms. Ravenscroft was quite lucid, wasn't she?, and certainly that presented a particular risk to Mr. Clapham. How could he be sure she wouldn't come to realize that it had been him, Norman Clapham, not Des Cheshire, whom Gianna saw in the Chicken Alley just before Billy Wonder's death? How could he know that she hadn't already realized that she had mistaken him for Des Cheshire, just as Justice Mariner had mistaken Mr. Clapham for Mr. Cheshire in the darkened club? Mr. Clapham heard Gianna say in court that she had left the Alley's back door unlocked, after she let Amicus the cat out, when the bar's owner generally kept the door bolted. How could Norman

Clapham be sure that Gianna Ravenscroft wouldn't add it all up and realize that, more than likely, it was him, Norman Clapham, she had seen, because he had slipped in through that unlocked back door? Inadvertently — or even on purpose, we'll perhaps never know — she had allowed Clapham inside to complete the tragedy at the heart of their *folie à deux.*

"And then, ladies and gentlemen, *then*, imagine how Mr. Clapham would have felt when, with Billy permanently out of the picture, Ms. Ravenscroft still regarded Mr. Clapham as nothing more than a sympathetic fop. After being her dependable shoulder to cry on, after all his tea, or flavoured vodkas, and sympathy, after, indeed, he risked a life sentence to win her for himself, she still was ardent for Billy, and eventually, on the rebound, for Mr. Cheshire. You might want to consider, therefore, that, having murdered once, it did not take much to provoke Mr. Clapham into murdering again, in the same dramatic, delusional way — in such a way that would further implicate poor Ms. Ravenscroft. In such a way that would make it appear that, even if Des Cheshire were acquitted, it was Clapham's former love interest, not Clapham himself, who had committed the double murder. And it almost worked, ladies and gentlemen. For once in his sorry, depressive life, on the cusp of middle age, Norman Clapham was almost a success."

৹৩৩৹

The party is in his honour, but Des Cheshire is on stage anyway, working with what remains of the Billy Wonder group — yes, now, sadly, there truly are three of them in the quartet — as they perform at this particular moment Paul Desmond's "Wendy." It is the special request — "our song," I have heard it called — of Justice and Mrs. Theodore E. Mariner, who sit right in front of the stage (a.k.a. Pervert's Row), sharing with Gaunt and Hussein a bottle of Moët et Chandon bubbly, sent over by the guest of honour himself. The middle-aged couple are seized with their own *folie à deux:* mutually squiffy on the fermented grape (*pétillante* for extra silliness), they feel a weary sort of rejuvenation, a little like callow teenagers after the school year's last exam. They hold hands as Des Cheshire toasts them from the bandstand, remarking that Paul Desmond composed the tune "in this very town, possibly in this very room."

"And possibly I ain't seen no royalties from it, neither, have I?" Jersey mutters. "Not a motherlovin' dime."

Mrs. Mariner throws the old cuss a suspicious look and changes the subject. "Ted," she says, "one thing I still don't get about the Wonder murder. Why a garrotte? I mean, that's a little exotic, no?"

"Well, if you think about it, it was perfect in the circumstances — another opportunity for poor old Norman Clapham to show how resourceful he was, or at least that he was no loser after all. For one thing, it was quick and quiet."

"So he could actually do it on the stage, while Jersey and the girl were in the bar."

His Lordship nods. "While anyone was there — Jersey, Kitten, Sylvie the waitress, College, who's my newest replacement as Jersey's dogsbody. But what makes it clever, Pen, is that Clapham made the garrotte out of materials from the bandstand itself, *inside the Alley*. That immediately expanded the possible suspects to anyone in the bar, and anyone who could have got in one way or another. And, as we pointed out in court, any number of people might have wanted a piece of poor old Billy Wonder."

"Still, it's almost as if Clapham wanted to get caught. I mean, in the end, the way he did it pointed right back at him."

"Absolutely," the judge says. "I'm pretty sure a part of him wanted to be found out — to show who really was the cleverest boy in the end. And the proof of his success would be that, even if the cops and Crown thought he did it, he had pulled it off so that they could never prove it. And maybe they won't."

"Yes, I see. It's like he's pushing it in your face, 'Who's the clever boy, then?'"

"Yep. And I suppose he might also have wanted to get the finger pointing at him in answer to a cry for help. As cliché as it sounds . . ."

At that juncture, Cheshire joins the Mariner table and, smiling his quiet smile, says he plans to take some time off, maybe even retire. He's feeling very tired, he says, giving some credence to Tommy's old Improvitron musical computer routine — which Profitt now performs with embellishments to suit the occasion, having come out of hiding and into a drug rehabilitation program recommended by Justice Mariner, based upon research by Nadia Hussein . . . soon to be called to the bar and Bay Street as the newest associate in the litigation department at Huffernan Sylvester.

As the Cheshire Cat saw it in retrospect, playing "Tunisia" that fateful night at the Alley had used up every idea he had and every idea he was ever likely to have. For that reason, he was glad Cueball Finklestein had caught it all on tape. Even though the recording sounded far off, hissing and spitting like a cornered cat or like someone made it accidentally in tourist class on an airplane, he listened to it over and over again, smiling and keeping time with his head. After nursing his wounds like that at his mother's old place in the San Fernando Valley, he cheerfully declared the Improvitron II the better man, and went straight to work for the company that made it, in Florida. A case of if you can't beat 'em, I guess.

In honour of old Des Cheshire's status as a Crown Prince of Cool, a Giant of Jazz, and Jazz Master of the Modern Era, they made him Executive Vice-President in Charge of Backlist and New Talent Development, but on account of his contacts he was actually just an A & R man, plain and simple, with a fancy title. Nobody up north saw him for about a year and a half after that, until one night, yes, he arrived at the Alley with another Rapster rep, and the two of them had brought along a new generation Improvitron, with twice the brains.

Oh, Lordy it was a bloody evening, more manhood, or machine-hood, lost than on the night at the Cherry Blossom when Lester Young played king of the mountain with Coleman Hawkins, Ben Webster, and Herschel Evans. Lordy. Not just evening; it went on to well past lunchtime the next day, the machines going head to head without so much as a rhythm section, and Old Jersey finally washing his hands of the whole business and leaving the Cheshire Cat the keys to lock the place up.

As you probably expect, the Improvitron III beat the capacitors off its old daddy, but even the youngster needed extensive servicing after-wards. Several new circuitboards. A dozen resistors imported specially from Denmark. Relays worth $10,000 a crack and diodes made of Iranian blown glass. (But it comes with a service contract, Des pointed out, two-fifty and change a month, depending on the pro-

jected daily "up" time.) At one point the bandstand caught fire and the old Alley filled with smoke, people coughing and wheezing and crying out for help something awful. They had to take one man out and lay him in the laneway. And there was a moment of genuine panic when Bones Whitehead tried to put the fire out with a bottle of gin, but then Terry Denver beat it to death with his coat. Downbeat *magazine said: "A real barbecue at the Chicken Alley: Out of the ashes, a new King of Jazz." But that wasn't exactly how the fire marshal saw it.*

Yes, once more, somehow, against formidable odds that include his own extravagantly bumptious personality, Leland Gaunt has persuaded a jury that Her Majesty wrongly accused someone of first-degree murder. And His Lordship has persuaded the presiding justice at the matrimonial home to pardon him for past offences, real and imagined.

Now old Des told the reporter: "Minimal compute time is how it does it. Those Micronesian microcircuits make it twice as fast as before. They're the smallest available. You need a strong microscope to even see them. It's the only machine with such advanced technology." The fire marshal ticketed Jersey anyway.

He was looking good, though, the Cheshire Cat was, very relaxed, sun-darkened now after the long winter of his discontent, thinner, a walking ad for his local jeweller. Got a condo in the Keys, he says, company car, part-time teaching gig at Florida State. The whole package.

Beats barnstorming, he says. Beats working for this season's Alpha Male. Beats looking over your shoulder every night and wondering who, or what, is gunning for you.

As for Yours Narratively, well, of course Jersey says he can't be doin' with no stray cats in his business all the damn time. Ditto Penny Mariner, albeit more grammatically, on the grounds of allergens and grandchildren. So, absent a sudden victory in the lottery of this boulevardier's life, my future is a little like that of Desmond Cheshire, Jazz Legend: uncertain. No doubt I will send you another postcard when I reach my next halfway house.